Finding Kerra

Finding Kerra

Published by Rhiza Edge,
An Imprint of Rhiza Press

www.rhizaedge.com.au

PO BOX 1519
Capalaba QLD 4157
Australia

Cover Design by Production Works
Layout by Rhiza Press

A catalogue record for this book is available from the
National Library of Australia.

ISBN: 978-1-925563-47-4

Finding Kerra

ROSANNE HAWKE

For Robin, my brother and friend.

I respectfully acknowledge the Diyari people as the original owners and caretakers of the land where this story is set.

1

When I returned to Australia last year, it had been the men's legs that shocked me—hairy, knobbly-kneed, muscly—all on display in shorts. But this July, when I arrived at Mulga Spring, Blake's station home in the Far North, I was freaked out by the dogs. *It was a bit of a worry,* as Dad would say.

With care I lifted the piece of wire from the front gate, hoping to surprise Blake. He wasn't expecting me until the mail run next morning. But I wasn't prepared for the painful screech when the gate swung open nor, as I pushed through to the garden, for the onslaught of barking and snarling dogs that instantly appeared. There were only three, but it seemed like a whole pack. When I stood still, they stepped back, but if I moved forward, so did they, baring dragon fangs as if they'd rip me to shreds. Maybe surprising Blake hadn't been my best idea. I retreated carefully towards the gate but one of the dogs circled behind me, blocking my way.

Panic drowned me as I realised the dogs wouldn't let me out. Two roved round me, while the third biggest dog stood a metre away, staring as if he planned to mesmerise me. The dog behind me closed in and nipped my ankle. It didn't take long to decide what to do next: I shouted, 'Anyone at home?'

A familiar voice yelled back from the house, 'Blue! Luke! Get out of it! Bow, ya mongrel! Drop!'

Two dogs disappeared like spirits; the one left in front of me flopped instantly to the ground, his head down, ears back.

'Blake?' My voice wobbled.

A screen door banged. My legs were shaky as Blake strode towards me. It wasn't quite dark yet and I could see his unsmiling face. It was humiliating knowing I hadn't started off on my best foot, but I shrugged that thought aside as my heart lifted. It was so good to see him; it had been months—his sun-bleached hair had grown.

He spoke to the dog first. 'Stay out of it!' Blake made a movement with his hand and the dog pressed itself closer to the ground.

'Here.' Blake was talking to me now, his voice softer. 'This is Bow. Put your hand near his nose and he'll know not to do that again.'

It took me a moment to obey, even though the dog seemed harmless with Blake standing there.

'Is he yours?'

'Yep. The head cattle dog here. He's trained to run the dogs like that—just doing his job, but he'll know not to round you up again.' With relief I recognised the humour in Blake's voice, and he put an arm round my shoulders as he turned me towards the house. I finally saw his smile that I liked so much. That familiar dimple at the corner of his mouth.

'Why didn't you say you'd arrived in town?'

'I was about to call when a guy said he knew you and was going this way. He's got a Toyota ute.' I would never have ridden with a guy I didn't know in Adelaide, but the manager of the Road House said it was fine.

Blake's answer sounded amused, but I couldn't read his expression. 'Everybody has a Toyota up here, Jaime. Though it would have been Matt Hall. No one else would come out this way.'

'Yeah, Matt.' The young guy had tipped his hat as he swung back into the ute, then sped off in a scuttle of gravel, his dogs grinning at me from the tray.

'C'mon inside', Blake said. I caught his gaze on me as he picked up my bag and I followed him towards the house. It was magnificent with the sun setting behind it, like a nineteenth-century station house on a souvenir tea towel. A wide veranda circled the house and plenty of sheds stood nearby. I could hear a steady thumping, like the heartbeat of something huge, and the clank and buzz of the giant pinwheel that rose above the house.

The sky was lavender, purple near the horizon, and as I watched, streaks of yellow and orange spread above me. It was different from any sky I'd ever seen, as if the sun had been weeping. The beauty of it stirred a chord in my mind that surprised me with its sharpness. Here I was at last, seeing the heart of this Australia I'd been born in.

I took a huge breath. When Blake Townsend had offered between-semester work experience—housekeeping on his family station with horse riding lessons thrown in—Mum had thought it a good idea. 'You'd see what the other half of Australia is like. Be nice up there in July—not too hot.' She sounded enthusiastic, even though I knew she was still worried about my getting over 'all that happened in Afghanistan' earlier in the year. Typically, Dad was more concerned about

Blake. 'What do we know about him? You'll be a long way from everywhere up there, so no funny business.' But Dad didn't have to worry—Blake was my friend.

Blake took me into the hallway, past the dogs, one of which licked my toes as I walked through the door. It was Bow; I recognised him because he was the biggest of the three dogs and had no black patches on his face like the others. I accepted his apology and patted him on the head, feeling the security of having a powerful ally. The feeling quickly went to my head and I reached to pat the dog beside him. I was rewarded with a growl and Blake's swift grip on my arm.

'Don't touch the other dogs!'

I jumped at Blake's tone, then he relaxed. 'Sorry. I guess you wouldn't know. They're blue heelers and they're not pets. Those two are Dad's dogs. Bow's okay, he's mine. You can pat him, he's smart and the boss dog but the others will rip your fingers off, given half a chance.'

'Fine.' I smiled, showing I was willing to learn, but my smile froze as I entered the kitchen. Another girl stood staring at me; not just *any* girl, but a fashion model out of the junk mail for R M Williams bush wear.

'This is Richelle.' Blake put my bag down. 'She helps out sometimes.'

Wasn't that what I was supposed to be doing? I wondered how long she'd stay. Instinctively I knew there wouldn't be enough room for both of us. She was staring at me as if Blake would need lots of extra help just having me around.

'Blake told me you lived in Pakistan,' she said.

No *hello* or *how was the bus trip?*

'I thought you'd be foreign, you know, black.'

How rude! I guess it was the emphasis she put on the word 'black' that shocked me, like it should matter. Blake's colour heightened as he watched my reaction, but immediately I was on home ground. She was just like Kate Sample, a girl at school in Adelaide. Kate used to say stuff like that when I first arrived.

I smiled at Richelle. 'No, I'm not black but I feel like I am at times.'

Richelle's eyes glazed over a little, probably trying to work out what I meant. Before she could say anything else, Blake's father strolled in. He was the legendary stockman, complete with the outback felt hat.

'G'day. You must be young Jaime.' He spoke as though he knew all about me, making me feel warm and welcome. He had an outdoor, sun-baked look about him, but even with the age lines cutting his face he was what my mother would call an attractive man. Blake's father left without another word and I had the impression that even though he didn't speak much, when he did it'd be worth hearing.

Blake picked up my bag again just as his father called back, 'Seen Kerra, Blake?'

'Nup.' Blake sounded as if he didn't care either, and I guessed there must be another dog loose. He took me down the hallway.

'This is your room, Jaime. I'm glad you came.'

And there was the old Blake I knew in Adelaide, smiling his old 'Coke ad' smile.

'The lights go out at eleven,' he said. I must have looked confused, because he added, 'We generate our own electricity.'

So that was the hum I could hear.

'If you're dying to finish the last chapter like me, there's an oil lamp.' He gestured to the mantelpiece and I gasped in delight.

'I had one just like this in Pakistan.'

He seemed glad I was pleased. Although *pleased* wasn't exactly the right word; it was more like *wonder.* I couldn't believe an old oil lamp could make me feel like that.

'Never thought anything would be the same, hey?'

I shook my head. 'Trying to find similarities just gets disappointing. Best to focus on what's here.' I sounded like my mother.

'Maybe you'll be surprised.'

I looked up at him, interested, but he didn't elaborate.

'Bathroom's down the hall.' He paused. 'We pump from a dam too, so you have to go easy on the water. Sorry.'

I shrugged to show it didn't matter.

'We'll start the riding lessons tomorrow.'

'Don't forget to tell me how I can help. That's why I'm here. That is, if Richelle—'

'No problem. She's Matt's sister. They live next door.'

'Next door? I didn't see any houses.'

He chuckled. 'Twenty kay as the crow flies. They have the next station, Bulcanna. That's "next door" up here.' He put my bag inside the doorway, then looked back at me. His green eyes softened and I felt we were back in Adelaide. 'Get some rest after that bus ride. Have you eaten? There's cold lamb in the fridge.'

'Thanks, but I had tea at the Road House.'

He gave me a sticky note. 'That's the wi-fi. When the satellite works. We don't use the landline much, it's an old party line. Don't want everyone knowing our business.' He gave a short laugh. 'If you need anything else, my room's out the back.'

Ordinary words but he held my gaze as if they were special.

'Thanks.'

And he was gone. Maybe I was just tired but I'd expected more, like a good talk, or a hug. I'd needed one by then.

At least the room had a comfortable lived-in look. The furniture was antique, dark and polished. It looked like it'd been dusted. I couldn't imagine Richelle dusting, even though Blake said she helped out. An old-fashioned fireplace, unused, was set into one wall. A push-up window was on the opposite side, with a fly screen that swung out towards the yard. I pulled down the blind and caught a brief shadow of the windmill whirring against the darkening sky.

To make the room feel familiar, I unpacked, putting clothes away and arranging my books on the bedside table. My sister Elly had made me a card with a drawing of her holding our cat Basil on the front. I set that on the window sill. The dressing table had an oval mirror and miniature drawers on either side. Between the drawers was a photo in a gilt-edged frame. The understanding eyes of a woman Mum's age looked out at me and again I felt warmed and welcomed. They were Blake's eyes and I guessed this was his mother. I knew she'd died but he'd never told me how.

When I arrived home this February after visiting Pakistan, I'd told him about being abducted, taken to Afghanistan and about my friend, Liana, dying there. He was sympathetic and he'd listened, but after a while I knew there was a closed door he wasn't letting me through.

It was another friend, Danny Dimitriades, who was able to go past the listening; Danny, whose grandmother also died while I was in Pakistan during the summer break.

'It hurts, doesn't it?' was the first thing he'd said. I was relieved. All my family, friends or rellies who knew about Liana kept off the subject of 'hurt'. Maybe they thought if they made me think about it I'd rush around the room like a mad rhino, breaking things. I did once. It was so out of character, guess it scared everybody, even me. But Danny and I cried together.

'It'll take at least a year to grow around it. I know—Grandpop passed when I was in Year 10. So you see, I'm an old hand.'

He'd made me feel more accepting of myself. He knew so much about life; a lot of it came from his family—they're so close—yet the rest came from just living and doing it with all his heart and soul. 'Just keep talking about it, that's what we do in our family. Talk, talk, talk.' He made a face and I laughed.

Mum took me to a grief counsellor. I didn't realise that my topsy turvy feelings were normal.

'Emotions are not tame,' the counsellor had said, 'so you won't feel them in any particular order. Some days you'll feel fine, on others you may feel angry, sad, guilty…' She had been right: I must have felt every emotion on the 'grief-feelings' wheel. Months later they could still bite me when I was least expecting it.

Now it was over halfway through the year and when Blake had said recently in one short sentence (as though it was a secret) that his mum had died, I knew he must have understood. Finding her photo here made me think this had been her special room—maybe a sewing or reading room, or where she'd sat with Blake as a baby. She didn't look like she minded me being there, and I shook my head at my imagination. How could a photo of a woman I'd never met pull at my heart strings?

After I changed into my PJs and snow-leopard-print dressing gown, I sat up against the bed pillows with my phone. The screen showed no-service, so I typed in the wi-fi password and sent a message first to Mum and then to Dad that I'd arrived safely. Dad's answer was immediate, like he'd been watching for it.

Glad to hear it, sunshine. Look after yourself and check in. Love you. I smiled at the concern he was trying to hide.

Then I took my research project out of my backpack. It was the draft of a story from Liana's past she had told me before she died. When I was younger, living in Pakistan, I'd understood Liana was quiet, even withdrawn. Being with her was like watching her gaze begin at the horizon, then settle on you instead. Even though I was only in Year 8 I knew she wasn't coping. I think it was the dreams. She woke up one night screaming. We heard her even from the next dorm. That was just before the terrorist attack on the school.

I was engrossed, considering how writing Liana's story had helped me through the last six months. Helping me cope with that grey, watery expanse that Mr Bolden, my English teacher, called grieving. At first I didn't notice the door of my room being pushed ajar. When I heard the little sigh, I jumped, thinking it was Blake, then my gaze travelled down to the light switch and met a child's pair of eyes, blue like a winter's clear sky.

'I didn't know there were any other girls staying here,' I blurted out. Not the best way to make friends but it didn't seem to faze her.

'Are you Jaime?' was all she said.

'Yes.'

She inched in then. 'I'm glad you're here.' She wasn't being polite; she said it as though my presence truly mattered.

'Really?' I wanted to ask why but this white-haired girl didn't seem the sort to speak unless it was already in her mind to say. 'What's your name?' I asked instead.

'Kerra.' She crawled on to the bed; not too close. She looked like a waif, perched there scrutinising me.

She pointed at my dressing gown. 'Is that a real skin?'

'No!' I spluttered. 'I love snow leopards. I'd never wear their fur.'

Her face was deadpan; maybe it wouldn't have bothered her if it had been real. 'What are you doing?' She edged closer, watching me as though her next breath depended on what I said.

'I'm writing a story. I'm just fixing it up for Year 12 English.'

The girl ignored the Year 12 stuff. 'A true story?' Even her interest was subdued. 'What's it about?'

'About a friend of mine called Liana. She used to tell me lots of stories and they made her feel better when she was scared. When we lived in Pakistan—'

'You lived in Pakistan?'

I nodded, surprised at how incoherent I sounded speaking about Liana. The counsellor said my grief was tangled with PTSD from being kidnapped. I didn't think I felt stressed at the time. Returning to Australia seemed worse. The questions were hard to field: W*hat were the terrorists like?, Were you forced to marry one?, Were they hot?* (That was Kate Sample). Even a radio station rang for my story. Dad said no. Y*ou need to get through this quietly*, he'd said. I was relieved.

'When did you live in Pakistan?' Kerra was sizing me up, a disbelieving pout on her face. I didn't look Pakistani, and I wasn't really, just *felt* Pakistani sometimes. 'Is that why you talk funny?'

'I grew up there, that's why I have an accent. We came back to live in Australia last year.'

She seemed satisfied, or maybe she wasn't as interested in me as I first thought. 'Can you tell me a story one day?'

'About Liana?'

She shook her head. 'One of her stories about Pakistan, or one of yours. An adventure.'

I blew out a breath. I knew by heart so many of Liana's stories that they came to mind as if she were still beside me telling them.

'No one tells me stories. And besides—' Kerra stopped then. Maybe she would never have said it if I hadn't prompted her.

'Besides what?'

'She's like me.'

'Who? Liana?'

Her head gave a slight movement forward. 'Yeah. I'm scared too.'

'Why?' I dipped my head to see her face but she wouldn't say, nor did she seem ready to go to bed. Maybe she knew that I didn't understand who she was and she wanted to tell me. When she did, it was all I could do to stop storming out to Blake's room to ask why he hadn't spoken of her. How can you omit a part of your life as important as that?

'Do you live here all the time, Kerra, or just in the holidays like me?'

'Of course I live here. I'm Kerra Townsend.' Then she added as though she didn't want anyone else to hear, 'I'm Blake's sister.'

2

The next morning I woke from dreams of a younger Liana running up our boarding hostel staircase in Pakistan, weeping. But when I hurried to hug and soothe her, it was Kerra in my arms, crying for her mother. I tried to shrug off the pall of the dream and walked down the hall to the kitchen. Blake was spooning scrambled eggs onto plates.

'I should be doing that.'

He looked up. 'It's your first morning. You can start tomorrow.'

It didn't seem the right moment to ask him about Kerra, and anyway, he started straight in about the horse riding. 'If you get your jeans on, we'll have the first lesson at eleven. Meet you out by the stables.'

I didn't tell him I'd ridden in Afghanistan in January, but I guess that was only hanging-on-to-save-your-life kind of riding. Blake was going to teach me western style. *The best for the land,* he said.

Kerra waylaid me on the way out to the stables. She didn't say where she'd been all morning, just surprised me by pulling my hand and saying I had to see the lamb. I followed her to what looked like an old dog run. A ewe stood in there, heavy from her wool, discoloured and bloody in places, hiding her lamb from view.

'A dingo got her. On the back. They always go for the backside. The dingoes get through the Dog Fence and then they kill the sheep.'

I regarded the ewe with compassion. I knew what the Dog Fence was: 5000 kilometres of fence designed to save livestock from dingoes.

'Then the flies got her.'

I stared at Kerra. 'Flies?'

'Where she was hurt, the flies laid eggs on it. She's fly blown.' Kerra said 'fly blown' as if she was telling me the sky was blue, like I ought to have known. My little sister Elly would have said, 'Duh.'

'Right. Fly blown.' I committed that one to memory.

'If you hold the gate, Jaime, I'll get the lamb.'

The sheep looked much bigger with Kerra in the run with it. Soon she emerged with the lamb in her arms like Elly held Basil, our cat. Except the lamb's legs dangled down to Kerra's knees.

'You can hold it if you like.'

'Thanks.'

The lamb lay passively, staring at me. So the stories about meek lambs were true.

'Dad'll fix it later.'

'Fix what?'

She gave a frustrated sigh. 'The mother sheep. He'll cut all that crappy wool off. That's crutching.'

When I finally arrived at the stables, Blake was already there. He was busy feeding the horses and didn't notice I was late. Horses poked their heads out of the half doors that looked onto the yard. A few shook their heads at me, as if they wanted me to notice them. Blake saw me step closer to one and he walked over.

'They're like dogs—make good pets if that's what you want or do jobs for you if you educate them right. This one is Dad's stallion. Got Arab blood in him.' He looked too big and feisty for me.

'Which one's yours?'

Blake took me to a chestnut gelding almost as tall as the Arab. 'He's called Cador.' His face crinkled into a smile as he scratched Cador's neck. 'That'a boy.'

'Cador sounds Celtic.'

He hesitated, then said, 'Mum named him. Her ancestors were Cornish—'

'Mine too,' I cut in.

'—Cador was an ancient ruler of Cornwall and guardian to Guinevere.' Cador snuffled at my raised fingers, then I patted his cheek.

'So you're a bodyguard, Cador. You look like one.' I moved to the mare in the end stall. She was pretty with a light brown coat. 'What about this one? Does she have a story too?'

Blake didn't follow me. 'She stays there. Richelle comes to exercise her.' His tone was clipped all of a sudden and I wondered what I'd said wrong.

Maybe he realised how he'd sounded, for he directed me towards the yard where a dark brown horse was tied to a rail.

'I'll show you how to rub down. This is Rainmaker.'

What a name! 'How come? She's not white like clouds.'

'It's not because of her colour. When she was born we hadn't had rain for over a year. We got seventy mil that day, hence her name.' He picked up the grooming comb. 'Brush her this way. She likes it. Then lay the blanket on, then the saddle. Always check the length of the stirrups. It's easy to come off if you don't have control.'

I never would have thought Blake knew all this when I'd met him at school in Adelaide. If I didn't know better, I'd have said this was his twin, although he still had that warm presence I'd always noticed at school. I could feel him in the room long after he was gone. Funny, he'd never spoken much of the station, his way of life here, the horses. All of which reminded me: 'Blake, why didn't you tell me you had a sister?'

He barely hesitated in doing up the buckle under Rainmaker's belly. 'Didn't I?'

'You know you didn't.'

He shrugged. 'It's no big deal. The subject never came up.'

No big deal? I frowned at him. My sister, Elly, was part of me, even if she did annoy me at times. I could never imagine not mentioning her to a friend I'd known for a year. Blake carried on telling me about how to mount and how to use my legs to steer and stop, while he led the horse round the circle in the yard. I suspected I wouldn't get any more out of him about Kerra, and, besides, it took all my attention to make Rainmaker do what *I* was being asked to do.

'Horses are like ten-year-old kids. They'll try and get away with anything if you let them. So you have to treat them like one—reward good behaviour, punish the bad. Whoa!

Now, Rainmaker didn't do what you wanted, so make her back up. She hates that. She'll respect you better now, but don't let up. She'll know as soon as you let your guard down.'

It sounded more like how to train dogs than kids, but it seemed to work on Rainmaker. I just hoped I could keep a firm hand. Whenever I didn't ride exactly as Blake had instructed, Rainmaker was quick to take the advantage, as if she was expecting me to weaken. Learning how to ride properly was going to be very tiring. The years it must take to be able to belt across the paddocks like The Man from Snowy River. It looked so effortless in the movie.

Blake seemed pleased with me by the end of the hour, and I was too, even if I had only trotted round the yard.

'Better not wear those sneakers tomorrow,' he warned. 'If you came off, your foot would go straight through the stirrup. You'd get dragged.'

'I don't have any boots with me.'

'There might be some in the cupboard in your room. A hat too. You're welcome to have a look later.'

Lunch time came and brought Richelle. There'd still been no talk about my jobs other than cooking the meals; nothing was said about looking after Kerra, which seemed a more needful task. After lunch there was discussion about checking the part of the Dog Fence near Mulga Spring, and Richelle was quick to offer help, 'since Jaime can't ride'. Then Blake said a few words to Richelle that I didn't catch, and he tipped her hat back with a chuckle. She smirked at him. It sounded intimate: the banter that kids often threw at each other at school. I hadn't understood it at first but learnt quickly that sarcasm was a form of endearment. The closeness between Blake and Richelle excluded me as surely as if they'd closed a door in my face. I was dismissed to 'have a rest', as if I'd need one since I wasn't used to outback life.

I smiled sweetly (I hoped) and retreated to my room, determined not to let Richelle bother me. Maybe Blake didn't play around and tease me like that because he thought I wouldn't understand, but I was surprised at the way it made me feel, as if I was new at school again and had no friends. I settled on the bed and thought about Kerra instead—a more comfortable topic. I wondered where she was. Not in the house, because I'd called. I lay back with a book, hoping she'd find me if she wanted. It wasn't long before her head poked around the door as if I'd summoned her telepathically.

'Come in.'

She was already on her way.

'You want to help me find boots in the cupboard?'

'Yep.'

The boots were in a box at the back just as Blake had said. Kerra pulled them out. 'They must be my mum's.'

I was thinking the same and wondered if I should use them. 'Do you mind me wearing these?' Blake obviously didn't, but I hesitated to upset Kerra.

She answered with a totally unrelated question. 'Have you known someone who died, Jaime?'

'Yeah.' I had to catch a breath as the questions came thick and fast.

'Who?'

'Liana. My friend in boarding school.'

Kerra turned her frowning face to mine. 'The one you told me about? She died at school? Were you my age?'

I took a breath. 'No, she died early this year. She was shot. In Afghanistan.' I said that firmly, trying not to see the slow-motion footage of Liana that often replayed in my mind; her look of numb surprise as she fell. 'There was a skirmish. We just got caught in the middle.' My eyes closed, seeing her hand still in mine, the jerk on my arm as she fell.

'Were you sad?'

'Yeah. At first it was like I'd had anaesthetic and couldn't feel a thing. My family thought I was coping well when I got home to Australia and I tried to keep it up.' I stopped.

'And then?'

'When it hit me it felt like the stars had gone out and they would never shine again. Like I was going crazy.'

'But it got better?'

I didn't answer straight away. People didn't ask questions like this. They often gave the subject a wide berth after a polite 'and how are you now, Jaime?' and I'd feel like screaming at them to just talk to me, even if they were scared of hurting my feelings. 'I guess it's getting better.' Even if I still cried at times for nothing, but I didn't tell Kerra that. 'What about you? You must know. Did you feel like that when your mum died?' Then I found out why she was asking. It wasn't just morbid curiosity.

'I don't remember.' We were quiet for a while. What could I say? I chose safer ground.

'Who looks after you, usually?'

'Mrs Crosspatch does, during school time.'

I stifled my amused gasp. 'Is that her real name?'

Kerra had the grace to blush. 'No, it's Mrs Cowped.' That didn't sound much better and I glanced at her suspiciously, but Kerra turned her serious face to mine. 'She has grownup kids in the city and visits them in the holidays, so that's why you came this time. Last year Richelle looked after me but I don't like her. I like Matt better.'

'What about Blake? Doesn't he look after you?'

'I don't like Blake looking after me. And Dad's too busy. Sometimes I go out with Dad and we give sheep needles or fix fences. I help him.'

'Is that where you were this morning?'

She nodded. 'We were killing a sheep.' My mouth gaped and she added, 'That's what we have for dinner. Sheep.' Then she sighed the same little sigh like the night before. 'Let's have a rest together. Can you tell me a story? About when you were in Pakistan. Is it green there?'

'Yes, it's very beautiful.' I could imagine why she was asking. There was only a small square of lawn in her outback garden. Even the plants were hardy with grey or white leaves. It reminded me of a holiday we had as a family. 'Once Dad took our family—'

'Who else's in your family?'

'Mum, Andrew, my brother and Elly, my little sister.'

'You like your brother?'

'Sure.'

Her eyebrows creased up as if she thought that was weird.

'We drove through a mountain pass with snow on each side to a place called Chitral. We could see heaps of snow-covered mountains rolling back like thousands of meringues on a giant cake…' I stopped. How could I explain the awesome beauty of the Hindu Kush ranges, the 'Indian Killers'?

'Is it a town?'

'There is a town and lots of villages. It's like a mountain kingdom, a lost one because it's so difficult to reach.'

'Did you meet the prince?'

I considered. I did meet a young man who was like a prince or who would have been a prince a hundred years ago.

Kerra tipped her head up, but still she didn't smile. 'You did.'

'A sort of prince, I guess, but the culture is different there. I didn't get to talk to him much.' I thought of the romantic story I wrote about him last year. But it wasn't really about him; it had been a way for me to process my feelings about missing Pakistan and learning to belong in Australia.

'So what happened? Did you see snow up close?' Her tone was so wistful I nearly teared up.

'That was the problem. It snowed so much, the mountain pass we came through closed. Mum and we kids had to fly out in a tiny plane to be safe, while Dad waited to get our little van out through the pass.'

'That sounds scary.' I gave her a glance. Any other kid would have huge eyes, not her deadpan expression.

'It was. Especially when the flight was cancelled due to the weather and Dad arrived home before us. He thought the plane had crashed on the mountains.'

Kerra watched me as I pulled on the boots.

'What was the prince like?'

'Like any other guy.' I tried to shrug off her question as I stood flexing my toes in the boots. They fitted.

Kerra pouted slightly. 'Tell me.'

'He was very kind and polite—good looking like Blake, except his hair was brown not blond.'

'Blake's not good looking. And he's *def-in-ite-ly* not kind.'

She said the word definitely with spaces between the syllables to emphasis it and I refrained from arguing with her. Most girls at school in Adelaide had thought Blake was hot, but then, sisters never did see the talent in their brothers.

An Akubra beckoned to me from a shelf in the cupboard and I tried it on. 'Come on, let's do something outside.' Getting Kerra out of the house would be good for her. 'Let's go for a walk, hey?' It'd be like a nature trail. Elly always liked stuff like that.

'Okay. But you have to tell me another story.' I was so flattered she liked my storytelling that I didn't notice the dulled passion underlying her tone.

3

Kerra took me to the dam 'near the house'. It was a bit of a hike but she kept me informed along the way. 'This bush is called bullocky, that one's dead finish.'

'Why dead finish?' I touched the leaves, thin like needles.

'Dad says it's the last thing to stay alive in a bad drought. When it dies it's the dead finish of everything.'

I knew the grey bushes were saltbush and I'd seen mulga trees on postcards. The wispy branches looked as if they'd been hair-sprayed into their wind-blown shapes.

'See these, Jaime?' She showed me the branch from a bush that I later discovered was native mistletoe. 'These berries are called snotty gobbles.'

Apparently she was serious.

'If you get lost, you can eat them. There are quandongs too.'

'Quandongs?'

'You know, little native plums.' She said it as if she'd already told me. She always said things in a tone to make me feel the dumbest person alive. There was a lot I didn't know and I began to feel like I had last year at school. I should have remembered that no kids in the city would have known all this stuff either, that this was Kerra's country.

The dam was ordinary—brown and low on water—but it looked pretty through my lowered eyelashes. There were wild brown ducks making figures of eight before diving for delights in the secret world below. The sun glinted on the little waves they made. Two little birds—either swallows or finches, I couldn't tell—swooped on the water as if it were an enemy to be teased.

'This is really nice, Kerra.' I took off my jacket.

She looked pleased. 'There's a rabbit. Look, Jaime!' I wasn't quick enough. Kerra went on about how the rabbits had to be killed because they wrecked everything. She didn't sound as though she believed in what she said; more like she wished the rabbits weren't bad and could be played with instead. It wouldn't be the last time I felt the urge to shift her mind off the current topic. I began a story.

Telling stories was soothing, even if Kerra's dead-tone questions at times were annoying. She lay back on the grass like a regular ten-year-old, her face upturned to the sun. At times like this she reminded me a little of Elly but Kerra wasn't as exuberant or happy as Elly.

'This is about a lake in the Karakorum Mountains in Pakistan. It's called Lake Saiful Maluk and it's near the top of a mountain, like an alpine lake.'

'Hmm,' Kerra said.

'There was once a prince of Persia called Saiful Maluk who visited the lake on his travels. He was resting at the edge, watching colours dance on the water as the sun set, when he saw a pari—that's a fairy—who lived there. She was so beautiful, and sang so sweetly, that he fell in love with her. He stayed by the lake every evening trying to catch another glimpse of her. Then one dusk he saw her bathing, and without thinking of the consequences, he stole her silken clothes. "Marry me," he cried, and the pari agreed to become his wife. You see, paris have no power without their clothes and must love the human who takes them.

'But the pari had a demon lover who wouldn't let her go. So enraged was he that he flooded the entire valley. But the prince and the pari lived together in a cave above the lake and escaped the flood.'

'Did the other fairies drown?' Kerra didn't sound worried and her clinical tone made me uneasy.

'Some say they can still be seen dancing on the grass and bathing themselves in the water, especially on a night when the moon shines its brightest. It's a magical place.'

'You've been there,' Kerra said flatly.

'How can you tell?'

'I could see the sky-lake in my head.'

I sat stunned. After a pause, I said, 'Come on. I have to get dinner ready. What would you like tonight? Italian lamb casserole?'

She didn't answer.

'With cheese on top?'

'Cheese sounds okay.'

We had just reached my room. Kerra had reverted to discussing rabbits: how Blake skinned them, how their innards fell to the ground in a huge plop and how Mrs Cowped made pies. I was wondering how to get Kerra off the subject again when she stiffened.

A door banged outside, I heard Richelle's laugh, then, Blake shouting, 'Kerra! Kerra! Where are you?' I didn't recognise his voice at first; I'd never heard him use that tone. Before he came striding into the house, Kerra had slipped out my bedroom window. There wasn't even time to ask her what was wrong.

Blake was heading for my door when I met him in the hall. 'What's the matter?'

'Where's Kerra?'

No *Hi, did you have a good afternoon? Are you enjoying Mulga Spring?* Just *Where's Kerra?*

'She was here a minute ago.' I didn't say how quickly she'd left. Hearing her brother shouting must have spooked her.

'I bet she was, the little brat.'

I'd never seen Blake so annoyed. 'What's she done?'

'Been in my room—'

The anger didn't seem to match the crime. 'She's been with me all afternoon.'

'She must have gone in before.'

'How do you know?'

'Because one of my cowhides has fallen off the wall. It was Mum's fav—' He paused. 'Kerra knows she's not allowed to touch them.'

I stared at him. What was the problem? Elly was often in my room; she even used my makeup one time, but I wasn't this cross with her.

'No damage is done, is it? Why don't you talk to her? She's a sharp kid.'

'That doesn't work. She never does what she's told—never has. Kerra's a pain in the butt—' He stopped.

Maybe it was the look on my face, or was it Richelle walking up the hallway towards us? Whatever it was, he blew out a breath, looking sorry. I couldn't help thinking it was Kerra who should be seeing that look, not me, but Richelle was taking his arm, steering him out the side door to his room.

'I'll see you later, then?' I heard her say to him. She barely looked at me.

I went straight to the kitchen to prepare the vegies for dinner. I didn't want to see Blake give Richelle any private looks. No doubt they grew up together, had a special 'thing'. I was beginning to get an uncomfortable sensation in my gut. Life's fine if you can sail through with nothing touching you too deeply, but real life isn't like that. As soon as something bad happens—a loved one dies or you find yourself liking a guy so much it matters who they spend their time with—all these weird feelings start festering. I knew I'd have to sort them, turn them over like a rock collection; decide whether to discard that one, put another on the top shelf, polish it a bit. I wanted to throw this one out and couldn't. I hoped it wasn't jealousy. Maybe it was I'm-being-left-out self-pity. Either way, it would need to be dealt with or I'd have a terrible few weeks wishing I could strangle Richelle every time I saw her. With an angry passion directed more at myself than Richelle I threw the potato I'd peeled into the sink.

'Jaime?'

I jumped. It felt as if all my thoughts had been on a screen above my head. Then I relaxed. It was Kerra.

'I didn't hear you come in.'

'That's because you were banging.'

I waited. With Kerra words didn't always come out immediately.

'Jaime, can I bring Sasha with me next time you tell me a story?'

Nothing about Blake, I noticed, as if his outburst didn't happen. I also didn't overrule her assumption that I'd be at her beck and call for stories.

'Sure. Who's Sasha?'

In her usual way, Kerra didn't elaborate. 'She's my friend.'

It was late when Mr Townsend came in for tea, but I had the food ready. I needed to keep busy and I was pleased with the result: lamb chop casserole and salsa (we had variations of lamb most nights) and peas, fried pumpkin, mashed potatoes with butter. Mum would have been proud.

'Nice potatoes, these,' was all Blake's father said throughout the meal. Apparently he looked after the vegetable patch when he had time, and Kerra did when he couldn't.

'Well, eat it all up. Stop playing!' Blake was staring at Kerra's plate. She was toying with her peas. I could sympathise: they came out of a tin. That sort always had loose shells on them. I opened my mouth and shut it again. I couldn't interfere and, under big brother's watchful eye, Kerra ate everything. At least her mouth did—I'm sure the inside part of her that decides things wasn't eating anything at all.

Mr Townsend seemed preoccupied at the table, as if he didn't notice. Maybe he thought Blake was doing a good job, but to me it felt as though a battle in an unseen world was in full swing. Later, I caught the baleful look Kerra threw at Blake when he wasn't watching, as if she had scored the last punch.

Kerra helped me clear the dishes. I had my hand on the tap when I noticed Mr Townsend standing beside me. 'You've cooked, love, I'll do these.'

He wouldn't even let Kerra wipe up.

Afterwards, Mr Townsend sat down to watch the footy since the satellite dish was working. Kerra crawled up on his lap. She was soon asleep and I thought how nice it would be if Blake picked her up and put her to bed. It was stupid of me to suggest it, but how could I have known? It wasn't so much the colour that crept over his face like it had that afternoon; it was more like I'd asked him to share his toothbrush with her. 'Is there a problem, Blake?'

His face switched to normal so fast that I thought I'd imagined it.

'It's just that she's spoilt. Don't let her fool you. She can get to bed the same as the rest of us—on her own two feet.'

He was smiling, it was the old Blake, but it also seemed as if he was warning me not to upset their order of things, the way he'd told me that first night not to pet the dogs.

4

The next day brought another riding lesson and a happy Blake. His face lit up when he first saw me. 'G'day,' he said.

He made me laugh. 'What a hick. You never said stuff like that at school.'

'Nah, but I like hearing you laugh.' He brought Rainmaker over. 'C'mon, you're doing so well with your riding, we'll be able to go anywhere soon.' His hand brushed mine as I mounted. I wondered if he'd noticed.

When he was like that, cracking jokes, throwing me compliments about my riding, I thought I must have imagined all the emotions from the day before. Every family had its bad days. Rainmaker was definitely learning to obey me; I hoped she would when Blake wasn't there. My progress earned me a ride to another dam later on.

'Want to come?' Blake asked.

I nodded.

'Sweet.'

I was having so much fun that I was swept along like leaves in an autumn breeze. 'Great, can Kerra come too?'

'If that's what you want.' I mistook his reluctance for wanting to spend time alone with me.

He came round to my side while I was still on Rainmaker. It was a moment before he spoke. 'I'm glad you came, Jaime.' I smiled, then he added, 'Only, don't mind...' He didn't finish, just reached up to take the reins. I smelt a mixture of horse sweat and Cool Waters as he helped me down. It took all my attention from what he had been saying. I liked it. Just as I'd always liked Blake. Here, he was home. At school he'd been Blake Townsend, whispered about in awe, but here he was an ordinary guy. Couldn't I still like him on his home ground with his warts showing? Everyone had faults. So he was a bit bossy with his little sister. I determined to like him regardless.

My decision was to be tested that very afternoon. The three of us reached the dam and Blake instructed me to give the edge a wide berth since cattle drink in it. I surveyed the sticky black mud, indented with hundreds of fresh circles, as it sucked on my boot and took a step backwards.

'So you have two dams?' Thoughts of the pleasant time Kerra and I had spent at the home dam filled my mind, even though she had gone on about dead rabbits.

'Nup, twenty. About seven water stops altogether, where we pump water from a bore and run it into troughs for the sheep.' He said all this as though he wasn't actually sure how many there were. My eyes grew wider and he laughed. 'We're talking almost a thousand square kilometres, Jaime, if you count Bulcanna as well. We run the two stations together. That's a 200-kilometre water run.'

'How many sheep is that?'

'Should be ten thousand. We'll be shearing soon, and then we'll see. Usually the dingoes get a thousand or more.'

'So there won't be ten thousand to shear?'

'Nup. Never is.'

Kerra seemed to be having fun, picking up tiny flowers. She'd left her sneakers on to avoid sharp stones and sticks. They were the washable canvas kind and I soon found myself wishing I had some too.

'I'm sorry the water's low,' Blake continued. 'We don't have a high rainfall. That's what makes it mucky, but there's nowhere else to go at the moment that's close enough.'

Right, close enough for me to ride to. I made another resolve: to learn to ride Rainmaker so well we could go anywhere, like Richelle could. Her mother probably gave birth to her on a horse.

'A penny for them?'

'Pardon?'

Blake was staring at me, the corner of his mouth dimpling. 'What are you thinking?'

I was about to say he wouldn't want to know when there was a squeal behind us. I sprung round to see Kerra in the dam with water past her chin, struggling and flapping her head from side to side. There was a frozen moment until I reacted and pulled off my jacket. A sharp sensation squeezed like giant pincers in my chest. Kerra was going to die. Then Blake's hand was on my arm, holding me back.

'Don't worry, she's just putting it on. Play-acting, to get attention.' It didn't look like playing to me and I shook off his hand.

After that I don't remember thinking. I threw the jacket down and jumped in the water. It wasn't deep but the sudden cold burned like fire and took my breath away. I swam up to Kerra and tried to pull her in. It should have been simple but she wouldn't budge. She could hardly breathe; the water was washing over her face every time she splashed to rise and gasp at the air.

'My sneakers…' She was gulping, flailing, swallowing mouthfuls of that dark murky water. Her shoes were stuck in the mud. I dived, but couldn't see and I surfaced again. After gulping air, I dived again. The water was too opaque. I couldn't even see Kerra. I rose again, worried my backwash would swamp her. Then Blake was there.

'Her shoes are stuck!' I dived again before he did, knowing I had to try even if he didn't. This time I felt my way down her body and legs, trying not to pull her down further. I could feel her sneakers—I fumbled for her laces but they were lost in mud. I felt another pair of hands just as my lungs began to hurt. Blake. Kerra and I were dragged to the surface. The mud didn't give Kerra up easily.

Kerra was in a full choke. I was coughing too as I helped Blake drag her, spluttering, onto the bank. I sat beside her as she rolled over and was violently sick. It looked painful. Brown muck spurted out and I tried not to think of terrible diseases kids could get from stagnant water. It was weird after that; even though she held my hand, no thanks were offered. The clasped hand said it for me, but there was nothing for Blake. They sat staring at each other. I couldn't imagine what they were thinking.

On the way home I asked him about Kerra, get it out in the open. 'Why don't you and Kerra get on?'

Blake shrugged. 'Nothing unusual, is it? All siblings fight sometimes.'

'I guess.' But I wasn't convinced. I fought with my brother,

Andrew, and Elly too, but it wasn't there all the time. Not like the palpable mood in the air between Blake and Kerra on the dam bank, as if that watchful truce was an illusion and their fighting was the real world.

That was when I began to worry about Blake. Dad's voice echoed in my mind: *What do we know about him anyway?* We weren't a couple; we hadn't shared on a deep level like close friends. Yet he'd helped me in Year 11 last year, had faith in me when I didn't have it in myself. The way he saw I was upset one day and drove me home. I'd never forget that. 'Don't try too hard,' he'd said. He'd been a good friend to me after Liana died, coming to my house in Adelaide, listening when I needed to talk about her. One night he'd even said he'd understood what I'd come from, being brought up in a Muslim country, and how I found it difficult to know the right way to relate to guys. He said it sounded a lot like the mateship of the Outback and he was happy to be my friend. Lately I'd found myself wishing there was more with Blake, but right now I wasn't sure. What if he had some quirk in his personality that didn't show up until he was home? Isn't that where you find out how a guy is going to treat you? In how he acts at home?

And what about Kerra? Did she have a disorder or just perceive things differently?

That night, after I sent an email to Mum about my life in the Outback so far, I sat up in bed in my dressing gown, reading on my iPhone. Kerra crept in to my room. She had a bundle in her arms wrapped in a baby blanket.

'I've brought Sasha.' And under her arm was a cat, young and very fat. 'She's a secret.'

'Why?' There was a lot to learn about station life, especially when no woman lived there.

'Because cats are only for catching mice in the sheds.' I could hear an echo of Blake telling me not to touch the dogs. 'But Sasha loves me, and I take her into my room.' A shadow passed over Kerra's face then, as if she'd said too much. 'You won't tell?'

'Certainly not. Bring her up here.' And I moved over.

'She's going to have kittens.' The tone was confidential—the way my aunt talked to my mother about 'women's business' when she thought we kids weren't listening. 'I saw them, you know, the tom and her. She growled funny.'

Weird what a paradox Kerra was. So much of life she'd experienced and in the next breath she could sound so fragile, as though I had to protect her—but from what? Blake's temper? The temper I didn't know he had.

'Do you get to play with anyone, Kerra?' Maybe she was in the company of adults too much.

'Sasha plays with me.' The child again. 'Everyone on School of the Air lives too far away. No one has time to take me to visit.'

'Would you like me to take you?'

'Can you drive?'

'No.' I hadn't gotten the nerve yet.

She brightened then. 'We could ride to Matt's one day.'

I didn't feel enthusiastic. How many lessons would it take before I could sit all day on a horse? The ride would take all day. Bulcanna was twenty kilometres away! I decided to drop that subject. Kerra settled down with Sasha in the crook of her arm, her thumb close to her neck. Then she reached out and touched my arm. 'Why do you wear that bangle all the time?'

'My friend gave it to me.'

'What's his name?'

I pretended to be shocked. 'What makes you think it's a guy?'

'A girl wouldn't give something like that. What's his name?'

'Jasper.'

'He's your boyfriend.'

'No, just a friend.'

She stared at me, disbelieving, but it was too long a story to explain: how Jasper exchanged my gold bangle for horses to help us escape in Afghanistan and had a copy made later.

Kerra touched my hand next. It was the closest she'd moved towards me and, just as if she were a feral cat I wanted to befriend, I held my breath. 'What sort of ring is that, Jaime? You even had it on today at the dam.'

I gently stretched out my fingers for her to see. 'I had it made in Pakistan. It's a copy of an ancient ring, the sort you give someone you love.'

'It looks like a hand.'

I took it off to show her. 'It's a puzzle ring and there are two hands, like the hands of friendship. See?' I pulled it apart. 'These two bits fit together and make the hand clasp.' Maybe it was the look on her face—such yearning. She didn't seem old enough to look like that, as if she'd never been loved and wanted to know what it felt like. Maybe that's why I did what I did.

'Would you like to wear half of it, Kerra? I'll have half, and you could wear half?' I could hear shouting in my head.

What am I doing? This was a copy of Liana's ring—it was her treasured possession. Mr Kimberley had the true one but he'd said I could have it copied in the bazaar to remember Liana by. Besides memories it was my only link with her.

Kerra didn't gush or say thank you, just held out her hand, her eyes the closest thing to shining, but not quite. It fitted her biggest finger and her hand settled back near her chin.

Then she asked, 'How did Liana get the ring?'

My mind raced. *How did she get the ring?* A lifetime of secrets and love. It would take too long to tell. I tried a short version. 'Years ago we had a music teacher, Mr Kimberley. It was a dangerous time for him to come to the school in Pakistan. We even had a terrorist attack there, some of us taken as hostages—'

She totally ignored the hostage bit. 'Why did he go, if it was dangerous?'

'His mother had died—'

'Like me.'

'—and he'd discovered that his biological father was in Pakistan, married with a daughter.'

'So he had a sister there. One he didn't know?'

'That's right.' Her perception surprised me, especially when it often appeared she had selective hearing.

'It was Liana, wasn't it?' She almost crowed. 'And when he found her he gave her the ring.'

'Actually they already had half each, but after she danced to save him and us from the terrorists, he gave her his half.'

'I wish I had a brother.' Kerra said it as though Blake had never been born and I was too sharp in answering her.

'You do.'

‘I mean like Mr Kimberley. One that’s trying to find you. Wouldn’t that mean he loved you?’

Words escaped me. What on earth made her say that? ‘Guess it would,’ was all I managed. There didn’t seem much point in saying you can only love a person you’ve met.

‘In fact, she’s a lot like me.’ It took me a moment to realise Kerra was talking about Liana again. It was as if she was finishing the conversation we were having the night I arrived.

‘Yes,’ she murmured, her voice a purr. ‘I like Liana a lot.’

5

Kerra seemed none the worse the next day after her ordeal of falling in the dam. Though, as I stood there at the sink, making coleslaw and watching her play with the chooks, my hands stilled on the grater. It struck me that 'fall' may have been the wrong word to use. How could she have fallen? Wouldn't we have noticed some sound, a slipping, a *whoa*-type shout? Or a splash? But there was nothing. Blake and I had been talking, then that sudden squeal of hers. It was bizarre; it was almost as if she'd *walked into that dam herself!*

I rinsed the utensils and took the dishwater to throw on the garden, an empty egg carton under my arm.

'Kerra! Let's collect the eggs.'

'Okay.' For all her near surly ways, especially with Blake, she seemed cooperative enough with me. In the afternoons she'd get her School of the Air sets out and do extra work, even though it was holidays. 'Mrs Cowped says I have to catch up before she gets back,' Kerra had informed me.

Kerra led the way to the chook pens. She showed me all the egg-laying places along the way: in the machinery shed, where I noticed Blake's blue car, and the stables. 'Speckles always lays her eggs in Honey's stall, but Dad gets them.' I wondered why. Was Honey wild? By the vague direction she waved her hand it seemed that the light brown mare was Honey, the one Blake sounded edgy about at my first riding lesson.

All the eggs were in the pullets' pen that day. I dragged open the corrugated iron door while the rooster strutted around the wire-meshed run, fluffing up his feathers, protecting his turf. 'Hold that door shut, he's trying to get in with the chooks,' Kerra warned. He began crowing and I berated myself for being so easily taken in as I marvelled at the simple earthy way Kerra accepted her world. Guess that's what prompted me to ask her about the dam; I figured a straight forward approach might work.

'Kerra, why did you go in the dam yesterday?' It was a long shot, but if she hadn't gone in voluntarily she'd stick up for herself, wouldn't she? Kerra didn't say anything until she was out of the pen and the wired door was latched.

'Eleven eggs. Look.'

I didn't answer her and waited. It paid off.

'Didn't mean to get stuck. Just to go in.'

'Why? The water was cold.'

'To see if Blake would—' She stopped.

I tried to keep my tone even as we walked to the house. 'That Blake would what?' Get cross? Save her?

But she didn't answer. Her mouth shut tight and I knew she'd say no more.

Later, after the lunch of cold lamb, beetroot and coleslaw had been cleared away, and dishes washed, I went to my room to check emails on my iPad. Today the satellite dish was working and there were emails in my inbox. I opened Mum's first. I told myself I was too old to miss my mum when I was only staying away for a few weeks, especially as I grew up in boarding school seeing her once a month, but her words of love made my eyes blur. She even referred to Kerra since I'd written I was looking after a motherless child. *She'll need lots of love, Jaime.* I could just imagine Mum saying it. It's what Mum was good at: showing love. I replied but didn't feel I should mention the dam yet. Then I clicked on Jasper's name. He was finishing Year 12 in Pakistan. The school year there ended in July.

To: Jaime Richards

Subject: Hi Friend

Hi Jaime,

Thinking of you and sure wish you could fly over for my graduation. Ayesha and Carolyn wish you were here too. We all miss you. Our class has been practising walking down the aisle of the gym to 'Pomp and Circumstance' banged out on the old piano. Would you believe Mr Kim knows how to play that too? Thinking all the time how you should be sharing this time with us. How are you tracking? I have days that have no colour at all. You must feel worse. I pray you have good friends to help. You'll be stoked to know I've finally learnt it's best not to hide my feelings. I feel better after I've shared a 'Liana' memory with one of the kids at school, even if we cry. Just write and tell me if you can't find someone who understands what you've come from. I'll always be here for you. Maybe we can Skype.

Cheers

Jasper

Tears welled in my eyes. Jasper was so familiar. We were in school together for ten years, even though he was a year ahead. We had shared so much earlier in the year when I'd been abducted on my trip back to Pakistan. He and Liana did all they could to find me, to escape. So much happened that I can't explain to many people here. Most are not interested, or wouldn't understand. They want me to fit in, live in their world without needing to know what mine used to be like. If I were still in Pakistan I'd be finishing Year 11 with Ayesha and Carolyn, helping the Year 12 class celebrate. I blew my nose and heard a sigh. It was Kerra. She was standing at the foot of my bed.

I regarded her, hoping I didn't show how she'd startled me. 'Why are you crying?'

'I'm okay. Just miss my friends in Pakistan.'

Kerra said, 'What say you tell a story? Then you'll feel better.' I checked her face for guile but she seemed to believe what she said, probably copying my words.

'But you need to do some school work.' The look on her face reminded me of Elly when she wanted me to spend time with her and I melted. 'I suppose it won't hurt, but you have to do some work afterwards, all right?'

She barely nodded and settled herself on my bed. Sasha too. Her thumb slipped into her mouth. Wasn't she too old for that? Disconcerted, I searched for a story in my head. If I knew Kerra lived here I could have brought some of the folktale books Elly liked.

'Okay, this is a story called "Prince Hamid". It's set in Persia.' Kerra relaxed beside me.

'A long time ago there lived a prince called Hamid. He

had a sister called Noori, which means "light". And what light she shone on Prince Hamid's world and that of the palace. She had been orphaned as a child and the Sultan had adopted her.' In the original story the young princess was really a poor cousin and there were three princes trying to win her hand, but I thought a shorter version would be best today.

'Prince Hamid was in the bazaar of a neighbouring city buying a special gift for Princess Noori when he saw a magnificent carpet. There were many carpets in the palace already and as he deliberated, the carpet seller said, "This is no ordinary carpet, sire. If you were to sit on it you will see why." Prince Hamid did as he was bid, sat on the carpet and immediately it lifted into the air and flew around the city. He was overcome with joy and bade it to take him back to the shop.'

'A flying carpet,' Kerra said as if she'd seen one herself.

'"I'll take it." The prince thought what fun he and Noori would have with it. He rolled it up and slung it over his shoulder. A seller of strange wares showed him an ivory tube.

'"Look through this, sire, and you'll see whatever you are thinking of." Prince Hamid was usually thinking of Princess Noori, so it was she who appeared at the end of the tube. His smile faded as he realised he was seeing her as she was right then and she wasn't happy as usual. She was tossing on her bed, moaning.

'"I need to help my sister. What can I do?"

'The seller of strange wares gave the prince an apple.

'"An apple?" the prince cried. "I need something to cure her illness."

'"It will, sire," the man said. "One bite will bring a person back from the brink of death."

'"Shukriya." The prince paid for his purchases, hopped on the carpet and asked it to fly to his palace. He flew up the marble steps to Princess Noori's room.

'"Oh, Noori," he begged, "wake up. You must take a bite of this apple." She couldn't open her eyes but she did open her mouth a little—just enough for Prince Hamid to drop in a small piece of the apple. He watched her carefully. Maybe she had to eat the whole lot. How would he coax her to do that?

'Then suddenly her eyes opened wide. "Hamid!" She sat up and threw her arms around his neck. "I was feeling poorly but now you are here I feel so much better."

'"I have a gift for you." He showed her the carpet and how it worked.

'She sat in the middle and patted the space beside her. "Let's try it right now."

'Hamid smiled. He'd keep the ivory tube for himself in case she needed him again.'

The sun was low on the horizon. It was time to prepare the vegies for tea and I turned to Kerra. She'd been so quiet I thought she'd nodded off and I wasn't prepared for the sadness I saw in her face. 'Kerra, what's wrong?'

The thumb came out. 'I wish—I wish someone—' and then she stopped. 'He hates me.' My hand was poised over Sasha, ready to pick her up to carry her to Kerra's room.

'I don't understand, Kerra. You're talking about Blake,

aren't you? But the Blake I knew in school was very kind. Why do you think he hates you?' I realised I had better think of different stories to tell her. Nice brother ones didn't make her more disposed towards Blake at all.

At first she shrugged and I thought I'd put an end to it, then she twisted the ring on her finger. 'It's because I'm bad. Really bad.'

I was horrified. This was worse than I imagined. Something along the lines of *he doesn't understand me*, or *he won't let me play with his things,* I'd expected, but not this broken, sad admission from a child who hadn't lived long enough to have gathered the amount of pain in her tone. I wanted to ask what sort of 'bad' but I didn't dare; I suspected this was the first time she'd voiced it. The words sounded raw and sharp, like bamboo shoots.

'You won't like me either when you know. Blake knows.'

Why would she tell me if she thought I wouldn't care for her? It was like she was testing me. I tried to shake off the oppressiveness of her words and I gathered her close to me. I could tell she was unused to hugging: her back was stiff and there was no returning pressure. Maybe her father was the only one who ever held her. I'd never seen Blake hug her and the image of Richelle with an arm around her wouldn't spring to mind. I almost cried, but stopped myself. Kerra wouldn't have understood.

She stayed in my arms, because I held her there, but her hands didn't reach round my back like Elly's did.

'Don't worry. I'll always like you, Kerra.'

I knew she didn't believe me.

Later, after Kerra tiptoed to bed and the generator fell quiet, I put on my jacket and climbed out the window. The doors and windows were never locked. So different from our place in the suburbs. There, if we left a window open, we'd be robbed for sure. The stars were so bright. I had never seen them with such intensity. Even in Pakistan in the mountains there were still lights of houses or bazaars to detract from their brightness. I sat in the middle of the handkerchief of grass, staring at the sky.

A step on the gravel sounded behind me. 'You awake too?' It was Blake.

'Yeah.' I whispered.

He sat beside me and in the silence there was peace in just staring above us. Then Blake spoke. 'When I was a kid, I slept in the room you have now. I'd climb out the window when Mum and Dad were asleep.' I smiled into the darkness; that's just what I'd done. 'The stars fascinated me. How small we are—how big God's universe.'

'Yeah.' It was just a breath.

'I used to imagine I could fly up there, sit on the stars and look down. I could blink my eyes and make wishes come true for other kids, my own worries would disappear. I would think good thoughts about everyone.'

'Up here is the first time I've seen them, I mean like this, so bright, so close. I've been watching for any that move.'

He chuckled. 'Yep, you can't see these in the city. Sure glad I live up here. Less complicated.'

'Hmm.' It seemed complicated here too but I didn't want to break the mood.

I leaned back, my hands behind me. Our fingers

touched on the grass. I moved mine away, conscious of how alone we were.

'Jaime.' He turned towards me. 'Thanks for listening to my drivel.'

'Ha, that's not drivel.' I was touched he trusted me with his thoughts. 'Anyway, thanks for inviting me up.' We stood, a little awkwardly, me trying not to bump into him.

He walked with me to the back door. 'See you in the morning.' He said it softly but I couldn't see his face.

'Sure.' He swung the door open for me. On the other side I paused and let out a huge breath. Then I tiptoed to bed.

6

My riding lessons were fun, not just because Rainmaker nickered as soon as she saw me and nuzzled my neck, but because it was a time of day that I had Blake's full attention—when Richelle wasn't there. It was also too early for him to have had any run-ins with Kerra. In those times he was the Blake I remembered in Adelaide, taking me to a movie or for a drive in the hills; the Blake who knew I'd make it in Australia. The Blake who could open his heart when he saw the stars.

'Do you like it better here or in the city?' I asked one morning.

'I like both. Flying School's great. I've wanted to fly for the Flying Doctors, ever since'— he sighed—'since I was younger. So I guess I'll always be in the Outback, but I don't think I'll make a pastoralist. Just being born here doesn't make you a good bushman like Dad or Matt. I won't stay here.' I knew he meant Mulga Spring. 'Too many memories. It's easier when I'm away.'

Guess that was my cue to say 'memories?' to get him to talk to me, but I didn't want to intrude. Kerra was on my mind, though.

'You're riding well enough now, you could come with us on the muster at the end of the week.'

'You're bringing cattle in? Or sheep.'

'Horses.'

I stared at him. 'Horses?'

'Brumbies. Dad's an excellent horse breaker. So's Matt. He and Richelle always help when we round some up.'

In the city I'd heard brumbies were pests to the environment. 'I thought they got shot for pet food.'

He nodded. 'That's why Dad likes to bring a few in before the shooters come. He thinks the brumbies are a resource to be used. They can be properly trained.' He said the last bit as if he thought I'd disagree.

Instead I was wondering how I'd go on a muster. 'You sure it'll be okay if I come?'

'Yep. You don't have to be in on everything. You can watch. It's only Dad and Matt who can really catch them, while the rest of us just head them off. Matt chased one for forty minutes once on his bike. Those horses have sure got some endurance. That's why Dad respects them.'

Blake chuckled, remembering. 'That day Matt landed in a creek bed. The brumby cleared it with half a metre to spare. Matt didn't have a hope in hell.' I laughed with him. Blake was great like that, sharing memories, relaxed, happy. It made what happened after lunch all the more difficult to understand.

I was coming out of the kitchen to throw scraps on the compost heap when I heard Blake shouting. There was Kerra's voice too, taunting. This time I was ready to intervene. I kept walking, following the sounds. When I turned the corner both of them were facing each other, their hands on their hips. Kerra looked like a miniature version of him. If they both weren't so angry it would have been funny.

'You know not to do that.' Blake's voice was still raised.

So was Kerra's. 'And you can't tell me off all the time. You're not my dad.'

'You need a hiding.'

'Blake! Kerra? What's going on?' I stood there daring them to answer me. Kerra wasn't crying but her features were set like stone and I thought of the insecure girl who sucked her thumb when I told stories. I stormed over to Blake.

'Why does a big guy like you have to argue with your little sister all the time? I'd really like to know.'

'Keep out of it, Jaime.' Blake's tone was alien. He turned to face me and Kerra slunk off behind the tank stand, like one of the dogs. The image upset me, making my anger turn cold and hard.

'How can you be so mean to her? She's just a kid. Who do you think you are?' I was shaking and even the red flush moving up Blake's neck didn't stop me.

'Who do *I* think I am? Listen to *you*. This is *my* sister we're talking about, one that I have a certain responsibility for.'

'There's always a different way to handle things—talking to her if she makes unwise choices. Having some trust in her.' *You're unfeeling*, I wanted to say. 'Can't you imagine what she's going through? She has no mother...' I hesitated. My anger was wavering. I never could keep it up for long. Perhaps he could tell for he explained as if I couldn't hear properly.

'That's exactly why she needs training. You don't

understand what drought means out here. No water means no cheque at the end of the financial year, no money for living expenses.'

He had to be exaggerating. 'What'd she do, drain the dam?' My sarcasm was no match for his steady reply.

'She left the hose on, while she was watering the vegies. All morning. She's been told to hold it at all times.'

'She wouldn't have done it on purpose.' Just as I said that I remembered her walking into the dam.

'She's a scatterbrain. A person like that could ruin our whole life up here.' He turned to go.

'Blake, Kerra is ten years old. She's only a child. There's got to be more behind all this than a tap left on. I can't believe a guy your age can be so strict with her and think you're doing your best—'

Blake swung around to face me. 'You can mind your own bloody business. It's the way things are done here. You'll up and go in a few weeks and everything will be left the same as it always was, so get off my case.'

We stood there, glaring at each other. I couldn't believe I was having this argument with him at all. The thought strangely calmed me, and I heard myself saying, 'All right, but I hope it doesn't have to happen again.' I flounced off to find Kerra.

It took a while, as calling her name never brought her, but in the end I found her under my bed. 'Come out now.' This time she looked as if she'd been crying, but I sensed she didn't want me to ask.

'How does the shouting make you feel?' I said instead, hoping she wouldn't freeze me out.

She sat on the edge of my bed. 'Blake always hurts my feelings, but I never tell him.' I bit my lip at the puny defiance, imagining the pain that must have been strangling her inside.

'Have you told your father how he picks on you, Kerra?'

'Nup.'

'Why not? He'd stop it.'

'He's not here all the time. Blake might hit me.' I was shocked that she'd think that. 'Besides,' she added, 'I'm bad. Dad might get cross with me too.' She thought for a moment, and I saw the fear, then the anger chase across her features. 'If I had a knife I'd cut Blake's nose off, then no one would like him anymore.'

I hugged her close to me; it was the only thing I could think of doing. Her raw feelings and words scared the daylights out of me. They hurt me too because I cared for Blake. How could he be one person to her and another to me? And how could such a little girl think herself so bad? Elly never did, only if she disobeyed Mum or Dad, but it didn't last long. Most of the time she was happily singing, eating or playing with Basil our cat. Kerra didn't even seem excited by special food. I'd tried so many ways of cooking lamb; even chocolate desserts. I only ever got a cool 'thank you' with none of Elly's exuberant passion. So far it was only the stories that Kerra showed any enthusiasm for.

As if she was following my thoughts, Kerra pulled away from me, scrambled under my bed for a few moments, then emerged to settle herself on my pillows with a furry bundle under one arm.

'Tell me another story.'

She sounded controlling but I was in a mood to be

gracious. After all, I wouldn't like to be shouted at by a six-foot brother who, to Kerra, must seem much bigger.

'Kerra, why did you leave the hose on?'

She didn't look at me. 'I had to find Sasha. She's going to have her kittens soon. If she has them where I don't know, Blake'll drown 'em. We have enough farm cats.'

My eyes closed. I chose not to comment on drowning kittens. 'Why didn't you turn the hose off?'

'I thought it'd only take a minute.' Then she looked up at me, a plea in her eyes. 'A story. Please, Jaime.' I stared into her eyes; saw the earnestness there, or was it fear? And then I understood. She wanted to escape.

7

There wasn't time to tell a story that afternoon as Blake's dad knocked, asking if I could go with them to help set up the shearing quarters at Bulcanna. Kerra didn't want to come so I left her in the lounge at her desk doing her school sets. I walked down to the Townsend's old house that had been used as shearing quarters the year before.

Blake was loading wooden beds and firm new mattresses onto the ute. The ute looked a bit like Matt's with a huge bull bar, aerials that would be seen above sand dunes, extra lights and even a winch.

I was uncomfortable with Blake at first, wondering if he'd speak to me after the way I'd had a go at him about Kerra, but he seemed relaxed. 'We do the shearing at Bulcanna. This old place is a bit run down for quarters now,' he explained, dumping more beds in the tray. I was given a rag to wipe the dust off.

'Shearers are pretty fussy blokes,' was Mr Townsend's observation. 'They have a union.' I had the impression he'd rather be checking the water run or the Dog Fence than carting beds around.

We managed to all squeeze into the cab of the ute, me

in the middle, knocking my head on a handle screwed into the roof. 'That's for turning the spotlight around.' I glanced up and Blake smiled at me. Amazing how he seemed to have forgotten our argument. It was still on my mind, forming a fog I had to grope through to reach him.

He gestured upwards. 'It's on the roof outside. For when we shoot roos.'

'You shoot roos?'

'Sure. The government has a quota, so we do some of it for them. Fifty a night sometimes. Gives us some pocket money.'

There were so many things to get used to. Blake even offered to take me roo shooting, indicating the rifle mounted on the ute wall behind my head. I doubted I'd go. I had seen enough guns during my life in Pakistan and especially when I was taken to Afghanistan last holidays. At the oddest moments a vision of Liana floated through my mind, the way she looked just before she was shot. We were running, hand in hand, to the safety of the fort gate—escaping. It was too easy to die.

The shearing quarters at the next station were basic but apparently passed certain regulations that those at Mulga Spring didn't. I stood at the doorway of the kitchen, took in the screened-in meat hanging space, the three stoves, freezer and fridge.

'Who does the cooking?'

Visions of me—or the horror, Richelle and me doing it together—crowded my mind.

'Chill.' Blake was undoing ropes on the ute. 'They bring a cook.'

I watched him and his dad replace the old spring beds in

the dormitories with the wooden ones.

'Come with me.' Blake motioned towards him and put his arm around me as he guided me to the shearing shed. 'I can just tell you're full of questions.'

'I was just wondering about the beds.' And that wasn't all I wanted to know—like how to broach the subject of Kerra?

We walked up the ramp of the huge shed and the smell hit me like a physical blow. Smells, more than any other sense, make me remember things, and that woolly, greasy stink—which must have been ingrained in the walls, the slats and bales—conjured up an Afghan carpet shop. I touched one of the rails as I saw a flash of the Peshawar carpet shop I'd been locked in earlier this year.

'See these, Jaime?'

I started, staring at the six shearing poles, all in a row, ready for a race to begin. The attachments and combs were on a shelf behind.

'The men bend all day, six guys will do a thousand sheep a day between them.'

My eyebrows went up. That many?

'They don't stop for much, get really agro if their quota of sheep isn't kept up. Their backs take a lot of strain. Hence the good beds.'

The sun hung low, shining weak rays between the rails, and I moved to the back of the shed, past the wool press. There was that lavender colour again, as though the sun had wiped paint-stained fingers over its weary eyes. Blake was right behind me. There were some things I could feel before I saw them; Blake's presence was like that for me. Just then I needed to have everything right.

‘I’m sorry about before.’ I was sorry about making a rift between us. I wasn’t sorry for sticking up for Kerra.

‘It’s okay.’ I wondered if that was his way of saying ‘sorry’ too. It didn’t feel like it and I almost reminded him that Kerra wouldn’t have left a hose running on purpose. I turned slightly to see his face and I left it alone. I didn’t want another fight just then.

‘It’s hard to tell with her, Jaime. She can do some damn weird things.’ He sighed then as though shaking his thoughts aside. ‘Anyway, what about you? What do you think about living up here?’ I turned to face him fully, willing to talk about anything safe right then.

‘It’s great, like a different country with its own rules. I mean, you wave at everyone you see, especially on the roads, and talk to people even if they’re guys or else they’ll think you’re a snob. It’s almost desert but it’s beautiful, the weather’s different and the land feels friendly.’ I glanced at him wondering if he’d understand. ‘I could walk anywhere by myself and I’d be safe. I’ve never felt like that—’ I stopped, surprising myself.

‘Yeah.’ Blake’s voice was low. He sounded proud and leaned in closer. ‘You’re so used to living in different places, you could fit in anywhere.’ I looked up. His eyes were shining and my lips parted as I smiled. Just then we heard a shrill cooee from Mr Townsend.

Blake didn’t move straight away. His face was centimetres from mine and I held my breath. ‘Time to go,’ he whispered.

That night I didn't get to think too much about what was happening in my head about Blake—like how I should reconcile my feelings for him and his treatment of his sister—because Kerra was hungry for the story she missed out on. It was becoming a bedtime ritual; the poor kid probably didn't get told many stories. I settled myself on the pillows and Kerra sat beside me under the quilt while I thought of one. Would she relate to living in a primitive mountain village in the foot hills of the Hindu Kush Ranges?

'This is a story from the Kingdom of Chitral where we had that family holiday.'

'Where you got snowed in.'

'Yes.' So she did listen, and she remembered. I'd told her that story the day after I'd arrived. 'Do you know what a polo game is?'

She nodded. 'Like hockey except on horseback. Matt and Blake play it sometimes.'

'In Afghanistan, where I was in January, they often use a goat instead of a ball.'

She frowned at me but didn't decry cruelty to goats like Elly would have.

'In this story they use a ball.' I decided to change the original story to suit her, making the main character Begal's sister rather than his mother. 'Long ago in a little mountain village in Chitral'—I heard Kerra's sigh as she got comfortable, not so close that I could put an arm around her, but closer than usual, a ringed-finger touching my bangle—'there lived the captain of the polo team, Begal. He was as strong and steadfast as the snowy mountains of Chitral. His horse was the fastest in the land and was named Bumburush, which means thunder.'

Kerra didn't snort like Elly when I told her the name of the horse.

I continued, 'Begal's team always won and his fame reached the ears of the king. The king challenged Begal to a game. Now Begal's sister, Gul—which means flower—was not only very brave, but wise. "The king is mean-spirited and cruel," she cautioned. "He will not be happy if you win." But Begal dreamed of winning as he prepared the black outfit he wore in polo games.

'The next day the horsemen faced each other across the field, their polo sticks pointed at the sky. The king struck the ball first but Begal blocked him from scoring a goal. After hours of galloping over the field with the clanging of sticks, Begal hit the ball through the goal post. The villagers cheered, but the king scowled and ordered a rematch for the following day. Gul was concerned but Begal was sure the king would finally see his worth.'

'The king's jealous,' Kerra explained.

'Late that night Begal had not returned home, so Gul went into the moonlight to search for him. She found him under a tree. At first she thought he'd fallen asleep, then she noticed the gash in his shirt over his heart. She wept over him. Then she pulled him over her back like a load of wood and took him home.'

Kerra's thumb popped out. 'She's very strong.' I stared at her. When I told this story to Elly, her eyes had teared up. 'Oh no!' Elly had cried. 'Her poor brother.'

'Gul is used to working hard,' I said, 'but she's very sad.' I watched Kerra for a response but she said nothing.

I continued, trying not to show how rattled I was. 'The

next morning the whole village assembled on the polo field. The king's men trotted out first. When the village players arrived, Begal led them, riding Bumburush. He was dressed in black as usual, but a scarf hid his face.'

Kerra looked up at me. 'So he wasn't dead after all? He got better?' Did I detect relief in her tone? Or not? I smiled nervously. Perhaps this story wasn't a good one for her, either.

'The king watched Begal in shock, then the game began. Begal played with his usual skill during the afternoon and amid the shouts of the onlookers, he finally scored the winning goal. Everyone thought the king would acknowledge Begal's victory and honour him. But he just stared as Begal reined in Bumburush. The whole field fell quiet as Begal unwound his scarf. There was a sudden uproar. It wasn't Begal—it was his sister!'

Kerra shifted in closer, so I put an arm around her with as little movement as possible. I was surprised because she usually squirmed away from a hug. Then I realised she was more absorbed than I thought. Maybe she was handling the story after all.

'"Why did you murder my brother?" Gul's voice rang out clear and steady. "He was happy and good. Today an untrained girl has defeated you, so it was not Begal, who was too skilful, but you who was too weak. Begal would have helped you become a better player than he himself."

'Bumburush breathed out in the cold air as Gul spoke again. "You may be a king but you are a very small man."

'Then Gul went home to bury her brother. The king blushed in shame. He sent an embroidered coat for Begal's burial and he never went to that village again, nor did he collect taxes from them. They say that a sister can be brave and have more honour than a king.'

I checked to see how Kerra was doing. Elly had cried at the burying bit. But Kerra seemed unmoved. Then I remembered. She wouldn't see the point of getting upset over a brother dying; she didn't even love hers. The thumb slipped out at my silence and she looked like Elly would during a long spell between courses at teatime. I wondered if I'd be able to keep this up: satisfying Kerra's appetite for whatever it was she found in the stories. What if they didn't measure up?

8

It was the morning of the muster. I was scared witless. What if I didn't make the grade? I touched my half-ring and thought of the adventures Liana and I had had in Afghanistan. Surely after escaping from a village on horseback in the middle of the night I could ride in a muster. Kerra was nowhere around when I woke, even though she'd slept in my room the night before. I knew Blake wouldn't approve of my babying her like that, but she'd dropped off after incessantly asking for more stories. I was too tired to comply but realised I'd have to be firmer with her or my life would be overrun with her demands. Though the rough time she'd had did make me sympathetic.

I'd just pulled on my jeans and Mrs Townsend's boots when her photo caught my eye. The warm smile was the same but I wondered what was behind the eyes. What would she think of the way Blake and Kerra treated each other? There was a certain strength in her features that made me suspect she wouldn't have stood it for long. It was like she was communing with me. Standing there, staring at her photo sure made me feel liable, as if I needed to make a difference. But how?

I was still thinking about it as I walked to the kitchen, wondering how Blake and Kerra would let their relationship affect their lives when they were older. An image of a twenty-year-old Kerra still sucking her thumb fled before the reality of them both in the kitchen. Blake was making coffee, oblivious to his sister as if she didn't exist. Kerra was calmly eating cereal, dressed for the muster. I hadn't realised she was coming too.

'I can ride with you then,' I said to her, just to make conversation. This wasn't an easy task unless Kerra was in the right mood. Nor was she the type to run up and give you a hug like Elly. Blake answered me, not Kerra. 'She could outride you, I'm afraid, Jaime.'

I stared at him—this was the first positive thing he'd said about Kerra since I'd been there.

He glanced at Kerra. 'But don't worry, she'll stick with you.' It was a statement of authority, not *Oh Kerra, do you mind?*—and I could tell by the pout on Kerra's face that if it hadn't have been me, she would have refused on principle.

In the stables I did what Blake had taught me: rubbing down Rainmaker, putting on the saddle, doing up the buckles. Everyone was doing the same, even Richelle and Matt, while the horses shifted their feet and mouthed on the bits like mounts in a Banjo Patterson poem. It was as though they knew what was coming and couldn't wait. No one spoke. It was eerie, like a ritual, and it was early; the sun hadn't even painted pink on the horizon.

As we mounted in unison, I could hear the words of the poem in my head: *There was movement at the station...*and felt the anticipation that riders must feel before a run. Blake turned Cador back to me. 'If it ever gets too rough, or you can't keep up, don't worry. Kerra will keep you company.'

Concern filled his eyes, assurance that I'd manage too. I was about to thank him, say I'd keep up no matter what, when Richelle called to him. The moment passed and he rode after her. Then everyone was off.

Kerra and I remained near the rear. There were times we lagged behind and I'd say, 'Let's catch up.' She'd grin and look as she does when listening to stories, before nudging her horse, Gypsy, with her knee and off we'd canter again. I didn't want to miss anything, nor did I want to hold anyone up. It wasn't long before my butt hurt but I tried to ignore it. Who'd own up about that when no one else seemed to have a problem?

Finally we reached wooden yards with a bottle-neck entrance. 'For the brumbies when they catch them,' Kerra said as we rode in. A truck stood nearby and Matt was riding his bike off it, down a ramp amid romping blue heelers.

'This is the camp where we'll sleep and eat,' Kerra informed me. I slipped down from Rainmaker and hoped no one was watching as I couldn't stand straight, let alone walk, and that was only from riding to the camp. The brumbies still had to be found, chased and caught! How would I last the distance?

Blake walked over with instructions and I put in extra effort to stand normally, like Richelle. He rested an arm around my shoulders. He was doing that a lot lately and I was wondering what he meant by it—just mates? Or more? I never saw him touch Richelle, except to tip her hat back in a joke. 'When we come onto the mob, don't try and follow us.

Those horses can be fast and mean. Just watch from a rise and if one comes near you, just head him off.'

'How do I do that?'

'Don't worry. Rainmaker's been in musters before, she'll know what to do. Just hang on and go with her.' I nodded. It seemed a simple thing to do. I held down the sudden panic threatening to wash over me. Blake didn't leave and I looked up. He was watching me, but I couldn't tell why. I didn't want him to see my fear, so I smiled brightly, stretching my aching back straight.

'You're some girl, Jaime.' His voice caressed me; it was a tone I hadn't heard him use before. 'Coming up here like this, willing to go on a muster—'

I didn't feel so special. 'What about Richelle?' She was handling things much better than me.

'Richelle was bringing in horses from the home paddock when she was five. This is her life but it isn't yours and yet you're willing to try. That's respected up here.' He turned to go then. 'By the way, don't worry about the aches and pains. It gets better.'

'How did—?'

'I started sometime too, you know.' He laughed. 'You're doing great.'

With lunch behind us, we were on the trail of the brumbies. The truck had been driven down by a Nunga guy, who was excellent at tracking. He was in the lead, riding Matt's horse. When Blake had said the tracker was part-Afghan my eyes must have shone. Anything South Asian never failed to move me.

'Steady,' was all Blake said. 'Zack wouldn't remember

much about his ancestry. He's not Muslim or anything.'

All the same, I couldn't keep my eyes off Zack—fancy finding a guy with Afghan heritage in the Australian Outback. Just thinking about him took my mind off my own pains, and it seemed like only minutes before he suddenly yelled, 'The mob's ahead, Tom.'

Mr Townsend gave a few quick orders before Matt sped off on the bike with Richelle and Blake following, but not before Blake turned to give me a wave. The expression on his face kept me musing while Kerra and I brought up the rear. By then I didn't feel so bad about Kerra staying behind with me; if she had my mother, she wouldn't have been in the muster at all.

'Listen!' Kerra held my reins so that Rainmaker stopped and pawed the ground. 'Hear that?'

The sounds of thunder underfoot, the crack of a whip, the barks and yells, the roaring of the bike. At that moment, I wished I was there; it felt as though I was grounded, missing out on a party. The noise grew louder and Kerra pulled my reins.

'C'mon. We've got to ride to higher ground.' I wasn't sure what the problem was but I managed to urge Rainmaker to where Kerra led above the track.

Then I saw them: a mass of swirling brown and black bodies, amid dust and flying tails. Mr Townsend was twirling his whip above his head and we could hear the crack even above the thunder of the hooves. Blake was on the other side, Cador twisting and turning to keep the wild horses within the mob. I saw some animals break away and there was Matt on his Yamaha, chasing them as if he was riding a circuit.

Three disappeared into the scrub, two he managed to bring back into the herd.

The mob was being driven down to the yards, but that was kilometres away and I wondered how they'd keep them all together. That must be the challenge which bush men like Mr Townsend and Matt enjoyed.

'Here they come.' Kerra's voice was higher pitched than usual and I turned to look at her, just as she pulled Gypsy back further. Was she actually excited? There wasn't time to marvel, because I realised we were too close. The mob was thundering past us and my hair blew just with the force of their passing. Gypsy broke into a gallop alongside and Rainmaker shifted on her feet—was it from nervousness or itchy hooves?

A brumby broke away from the mob, then another followed, quite near me. Whether I wanted to give chase or not, I had no choice as Rainmaker took off, straining and galloping after them. I remembered Blake's words: *Stay with her*. And I tried.

The rogue brumbies were heading away from the mob towards the denser salt bush. Rainmaker followed them at a full gallop. Even though I'd ridden in Afghanistan, it had been nothing like this. Rainmaker twisted and turned, shook her head. If I hadn't known better, I'd have sworn she was trying to be rid of me so she could chase the brumbies at a speed she was used to. Instantly the wild horses twisted to the right and almost turned back on themselves. And that was when Rainmaker and I parted company. There was no way I could hold on with her spiralling around to follow them under the low mulga trees.

My backside was sliding off one side of the saddle. Then

my foot slipped out of the stirrup. I should have hung on, but dropping off seemed a better option than being thrown. The first thump on the ground knocked all the wind out of my lungs, as if I'd been hit on the back with a cricket bat. Then I rolled. I thought I'd never stop and when finally I was flat on my back, I could barely breathe, nor did I dare move. Thoughts of wheelchairs and disability parking lots filled my mind until I found the courage to start moving fingers and toes.

It was ages before I managed to sit up. Nothing felt broken, not even a rib, but I knew I'd be sore. Even then I had no idea how lucky I was, how I could've been dragged or knocked out by one of the rocky outcrops. It was getting late and no horse in sight. We must have travelled quite a distance; there was Buckley's (as Dad would say) of me finding a way back to camp. I crawled to a mulga tree and sat against one of the trunks; at least I'd have a bit of shelter.

It was eerie being in an expanse of dark land and sky, like the scrub was waiting to see how I'd respond. A wind had sprung up; it was close on dusk and getting colder when I heard the howls of dingoes. There was a rustle in the grass behind me. I turned my head and winced. Everything felt sore. It wasn't Rainmaker as I'd hoped. Only a few metres away stood a red kangaroo and it knew I was there. I managed to pull myself up, holding onto small branches. The kangaroo stood higher too. It was huge. Would it attack me? I'd heard gruesome stories about men being slit from top to bottom by their claws. It dropped to its haunches again and moved away, grazing.

Another howl, closer this time. Should I try to climb?

The mulga didn't look as if it would hold me. And I couldn't run: everything hurt. A chorus of howls started up. I was determined not to cry, but every sound echoing in the bush around me was amplified by my fear.

Then came a snort. I called, 'Rainmaker!' But it wasn't. Not a brumby either.

It was Matt. He had Kerra with him. 'You or'right?' was his offhand comment as if he regularly found people who fell off horses.

'Yeah.' What a relief. 'How did you find me?'

'Rainmaker.' Like Mr Townsend, it seemed Matt didn't say much. I prompted him. 'What did she do?'

'Zack saw her chasing her tail in the bush. Without you. So we knew you'd be around.'

I grimaced. 'Yeah.' I'd never felt more like the 'new chum' as I did then, and I decided a little defence was in order. 'She tried to chase a brumby.'

Matt grunted as he dismounted. 'Spooked, more likely.'

Kerra piped up then. 'We found you first.' She sang the words like any other ten-year-old and she jumped off Gypsy to skip around Matt as he took two blankets from his horse.

'C'mon, Kerra, help me find some kindling for a fire.'

'Shouldn't we go back?' I watched Kerra, absorbed in her task. I hadn't seen her look that happy at the homestead.

'No need. Zack's still catching Rainmaker, and if he doesn't, she might come back to where she dropped you. Then we'll return.'

'Won't the others be worried?'

'Nah. I know this part of the country real well. They know that too. I'm often out here to check the waterholes for campers.'

I didn't understand what he was talking about and it must have shown as he added, 'Sheep won't drink where there's people camped. They'll die of thirst within metres of the dam.'

'Oh.' I digested this startling piece of bush lore. At least he didn't talk to me like Kerra did as though I should've known.

Soon Matt had the fire burning (it was a five-dog night, he said) and I sat there almost mesmerised as I stared into the different colours fanning against the dark sky, my back aching and my mind blank. Kerra sat in my lap and I put the blanket Matt had handed me round us both. Matt stayed on the other side of the fire. He had that aura of 'outback mateship' stamped all over him. It made me feel safe. I wanted to ask him lots of questions, about Blake, Kerra, the Townsends; I knew he'd give me an honest answer. But I couldn't, not with Kerra there, leaning against me, hanging onto all that was going on.

'Jaime, tell us a story.'

Matt tuned in then. 'Story?'

'She tells stories. She's as good as someone on TV.' I hoped she wasn't thinking of Playschool.

'That'd be nice.' Matt actually sounded interested. 'Nungas told stories round the campfire. It's the way they passed stuff on, the way they taught the mob.' He made it sound like an important art that was dying.

'C'mon, Jaime. You said you knew lots of stories.'

I sighed at Kerra's bossy tone. 'What sort of story?'

'One where a hero saves someone.' I regarded the top of her head, wondering if she did care and if stories could truly heal the hurt.

Even Matt was looking expectant through the smoke of the fire.

So I told them about Queen Scheherazade and how she made up stories for 1001 nights to stay alive.

'Why would she have to stay alive?' Kerra asked.

I took a deep breath. 'The king's wife left him and he was so sad and angry that he married a girl each day and had her beheaded the next morning.'

'That's random.' Matt looked appalled, but Kerra was quiet.

'Yes, but Scheherazade was the vizier's daughter and she had a plan to save the girls who were left. She offered to marry the king. The first night he came to her tent she asked if she could tell a story. The king liked stories so he agreed. Scheherazade was so good at telling stories that she had the king enthralled all night and when the sky lightened in the east, he said, "Quickly, finish it off, it's time for your beheading."

'"Sire," she said, "the story will be ruined if I rush the ending. Please may I finish it when you come tonight? Just one more day."

'The king finally agreed, so that night she finished the story and started another—'

'And the king wanted to hear the ending of that one too?' Kerra asked.

'Absolutely. Finally after 1001 nights of telling stories, Scheherazade had had enough.

'"Sire, I am your wife, I have born you two sons, surely you can lift this threat of death from me?"

"My piari," the king replied, "don't you know I have

grown to love you? No longer do I want to kill anyone. Your stories have healed my mind and my heart.'"

At the end, Kerra did something I'd never noticed her do before: she gasped.

9

After the storytelling I felt like packing it in for the night, but Kerra decided to fill Matt in on some details of my life.

'Jaime was a hostage twice. Once in Pakistan when she was younger. There was an attack on her school. And again this year, she was kidnapped, weren't you, Jaime?' She said it as if she'd done high school history and knew all about sub-continent wars.

I nodded dumbly under Matt's respectful gaze.

'Tell us what it was like being a hostage when you were little,' Kerra urged.

I looked up, surprised that she'd remembered that and embarrassed that Matt may be bored. But he was leaning forward.

'It was years ago. I was in Year 8,' I said, but both Matt and Kerra waited for me to keep going. I sighed. 'We girls were kept in a dark little room in a Mughal caravanserai, like an ancient motel for travellers and their camels or horses. I climbed up the rough bricks to the barred window to get a look outside sometimes.'

'What did you see?' Matt asked.

'Snow-topped mountains. There was a river that lapped

up against the walls of the place. We only knew that because we could hear it at night. We could hear the men—'

Kerra butted in. I'd never seen her do that before either. 'But early this year her friend died in Afghanistan when they were kidnapped.'

I flinched before I heard Matt's indrawn breath. 'Did that really happen? And your friend—' He glanced at Kerra.

I nodded.

'I'm sorry,' he said.

'Jaime's had lots of adventures. Tell us some more.'

Kerra made me feel like I'd betrayed a confidence.

Matt came to my rescue. 'Must be time for you to turn in, Kerra. Jaime will be tired from falling off Rainmaker.'

Kerra closed her lips into a pout. At times I wondered if she couldn't feel empathy for others. Surely she was tired too; I could feel her growing heavier as I talked, so I laid her by the fire with the blanket tucked round her.

'You've been through a lot it sounds like.' Matt paused. 'Do you want to talk about your friend?'

I bit my lip. It felt good to have someone ask that. And I began telling him everything: how I was kidnapped by accident in January and my friends—Jasper, Liana and Sonya—found me in a Peshawar carpet shop, and how we were taken into Afghanistan to keep us safe but finally got away.

'Some of the freedom fighters were good guys looking after the people, some were just terrorists. We met both.'

'Did the terrorists kill your friend?' His voice was gentle.

'We were escaping, holding hands. I don't know if a guy was aiming at us or if it was a stray bullet.'

Matt groaned softly. I looked up to find him regarding me from the other side of the fire. It was burning lower now and I edged closer to the warmth. 'Must have been strange coming back from a place like that.'

I nodded. 'Pakistan was where I was brought up. I knew it, loved it.' I remembered my speech at a school dinner last year. 'Back here it was like dropping my life in the dark and not being able to find it.'

Matt nodded. 'Lots of different ways of doing things in those countries. Cut your hands off for stealing, I heard.'

'Sometimes.' There was so much more I could have said about Pakistan: its ancient timelessness, its beauty and mystery, the generosity and hospitality of the people. But I'd learnt people here weren't always interested in that face of Pakistan.

'You used to Australia now?' No one had asked me that for a long time either, and I had to think.

'Yeah, I reckon. I've been here eighteen months. There's still times when I do the wrong thing or moments when I feel like I can hear music other people can't.' I didn't expect Matt to understand that but I underestimated the wisdom that comes to people who spent a lot of time on their own.

'Know what you mean,' was all he said.

'Can I ask you something, Matt?'

He shifted in his blanket. 'Fire away.'

'Do you know that Blake picks on Kerra?'

'Is he still?'

'He always did?'

Matt didn't answer that, instead, he said, 'They've had a hard time of it, the Townsends. They've come out of it as good as can be expected, I reckon.'

I wanted to talk about the rights and wrongs of bullying your little sister, but I sensed I wouldn't get far. Instead, I asked, 'What happened?'

Maybe Matt was tired, but more likely it was tied up with not talking about a mate when he wasn't there. Commendable, but annoying when I was desperate to know. He was quiet for ages so that I began to think he hadn't heard me after all, until he stretched out by the fire and finally spoke.

'You'll have to ask Blake yourself. It's to do with his mother. That's only my opinion, mind you, but he is the one who needs to tell you. God knows he needs to tell someone; it may as well be you.'

The sun was rising by the time we arrived at the muster camp. Rainmaker hadn't turned up as Matt predicted so Kerra let me ride Gypsy while she rode in front of Matt on his horse. When I protested, he said it wasn't far. I had a lot to learn about the rules between the sexes in the Outback. If Matt was half-dying, he wouldn't have let me have the extra weight of Kerra. I chose to accept it as the respect I thought it meant. I was used to that in Pakistan.

Matt's 'not far' was a lot further than I realised and I was embarrassed to have been a bother to everyone. I was glad it was early; glad that the first one to greet me was only Bow. Matt let Kerra down while I managed to climb off with the grinning blue heeler pawing at me.

'Hey, Bow, did you miss me?'

He nearly knocked me over, and as I patted the rippling

muscles in his upper front torso, I was glad to be on the right side of him. When I met him in the Townsend's yard that first night I never dreamed he'd be all over me like prickly heat one day.

Blake was there then, and Richelle. She didn't look pleased, more like she'd hoped I'd fallen down a thousand-foot bore hole. Blake was all care and concern, and under his questioning I remembered all my bruises.

'I think I've pulled muscles in my back. I came off Rainmaker when she swerved to chase the brumbies. Did she turn up?'

'Yep. Last night. But there was no point looking for you in the dark.'

Richelle cut in then. 'Besides, we knew Matt would be with you.'

I don't think I imagined it: she sounded bitchy and I checked how Blake took it. Guys I knew at school would get uptight if a girl they liked spent the night in the bush with another guy, but Blake seemed fine. Guess he knew his mate, or—horrible thought—he didn't care enough for it to bother him. It was beginning to matter what he thought about me and I wasn't sure I enjoyed being in another's power like that.

Zack turned up and was introduced. For an instant I was shy; he was tall, good looking like guys I'd seen in Afghanistan, though with a broader nose. I remembered in time that Zack wasn't Afghan in the traditional sense. I shook his hand and thanked him for catching Rainmaker the way I would have done to Matt. 'No worries,' was all Zack said at first but he stood there in front of me with more to say. Apparently Blake had told him I'd been in Afghanistan earlier in the year.

'I live in town,' he finally said. 'Would ya like to visit? My mum would like to see ya. After the muster?'

It was painfully obvious he didn't invite many girls home and how to do it without sounding like he was asking for a date tied him in knots. I'm sure if his skin was paler he'd have a pink blush rising up his neck.

Blake was enjoying it too and with a smirk towards me as I nodded, he said, 'Sure thing, mate. I'll bring her.'

With all my aches and pulled muscles, Blake or Matt wouldn't hear of my riding with them that day to catch more brumbies. They'd only caught six the day before, which, as Matt said, wasn't a bad haul considering what cunning brutes wild horses were. That's a subtle translation of what Matt really called them.

It was Matt who took me to the yards for a look. As we approached, the brumbies rushed to the other side of the fence, kicking and eating the dust (Matt's words). I kept seeing the huge mob thundering through the scrub yesterday, and here were only six!

'They're hard to catch,' Matt explained. 'Even the professionals up north, who do it for a living, only get seventy in a five-day muster.'

I wondered how they could be tamed. Four of the horses were huddled almost on top of each other in the furthermost corner of the yard. The other two were running at the fence, banging their heads and torsos on the steel rails. 'Do they get out?'

'Not often. We've strengthened the yards. They'll kick down wooden fences.'

'How will you get them home?' I thought of the answer at the same time he gave it.

'The truck. We'd lose them in the bush otherwise.' Matt put a boot on the bottom rail. 'Blake's father can change these mongrels into stock horses that'll eat out of his hand.'

I didn't butt in with questions as it dawned on me that I'd passed some sort of test the night before and now I was being offered a friendship—mateship—that would probably never be spoken about. A warm security soaked through me and I knew that Matt would be there when I needed him. He explained that people used to break the horse's spirit, but Mr Townsend used a control rope with gentle talking and touching. 'A horse will never forget a hard breaking, they'll kick and bite, but with Mr Townsend's way, they have no fear of people.'

'Matt.' He was watching the brumbies quietening down, though a few still scrambled for the corner. He glanced down at me.

'Thanks.' I had to say it but I didn't expect him to know why.

He surprised me. 'Think nothing of it.' Despite his words, I knew it meant a great deal to a guy like Matt. I felt I'd managed to slip under the gate of a fortified castle.

While I was 'in' I'd ask Matt another question.

'Do you think Richelle minds me coming here for work experience? Would she rather have done the job?' I held my breath, unsure if I'd like what he said. I couldn't imagine Matt saying anything negative about his sister, yet she hadn't exactly rolled out the red carpet for me.

'Don't let Richelle get to you. She doesn't like change. Or sharing. She'll come good. She just doesn't think that anyone from such a different background would know what was best for—well, for Blake.'

'Was she Blake's girlfriend once?' I had to ask that, even though I knew she couldn't be now—for why would he ask me to come?

'Nah. They're mates. Always have been. Always will be.'

He held my gaze as he spoke and I recognised the care in his eyes. I knew he wasn't just talking about them. In that moment I came to understand Blake's friendship with Richelle.

The night we returned to the Townsends' house I was sent in the truck with Zack and, of course, Kerra wanted to go with me. I thought the muster would have worn Kerra out, but she chatted constantly. Being away from home turned her into a regular ten-year-old. When we drove off Matt's eyebrows were perched high, like *you've really scored with the kid.* Yet, he didn't seem jealous, and I was reminded of the tower of a caravanserai, how it shelters you in a storm or a battle. I could tell Matt was one of those people who believed in special places in the heart. No doubt he knew he had one in Kerra's and felt secure enough to know that it couldn't be replaced, that Kerra's heart would grow bigger for me.

Her father and Matt were the only other people Kerra seemed to care about. Even Bow, I noticed, only paid her attention when Blake wasn't around. It was weird how Bow sensed that Blake wouldn't approve. I watched Kerra waving to Matt and then caught her look as she glanced up at me. It seemed like adoration, but it was hungry and pleading too, like an addict who's run out of chocolate and knows you have some. I wasn't fooled; I knew why she came with me. It was the stories: they took her somewhere else.

Kerra was already tucked into her bed and I was about to put the light out when she said my name. Elly did that to keep me on her bed longer, as if it were life or death. I stood at the door, wondering if this was a false alarm and Kerra would drop off after all, but she rolled onto her back.

'Jaime? When you were talking to Matt at the campfire, did it make you feel better?'

So she'd heard us. I thought she'd been asleep. This wouldn't keep till later and I sat on the bed. 'Kerra, when you talk about things, get them out in the open, it does help. It's a very brave thing to do, like facing a big shadow in a cave. It might look like a dragon's shape, but until you take a torch and go and see that it's only the moonlight shining on a funny-shaped rock, you'll always be scared of it.' Even as I was talking, I still had no idea of the size of Kerra's dragon, or maybe I wouldn't have been so flippant with my solution.

She sat up then, and I saw the first glimmer of hope in her face that I'd seen. 'Liana told you a story about her and her brother, didn't she?'

'Yes, she grew brave when she had to save him and her friends.'

'She did it by dancing.'

'I guess.' There was so much more—too much to explain.

'And telling you about it made her feel better.'

'Possibly.' I didn't know where this was going.

'And the stories you tell me—they're for feeling better too.'

I sighed. It was *her* story she needed to tell. 'They're just folktales.'

Her face had a stubborn look about it then. 'No, they're not. You said stories help, to talk is to help. They're true, and they can happen to me as well.'

I stared at her. It shouldn't have been such a surprise; I'd begun to suspect she was making more of the stories than any regular kid would. Did I just think that? Wasn't Kerra a regular person?

Then her face softened. 'Was it brave of me to tell you that Blake is always cross with me?'

I drew her to me then. 'Yes, it was. And that's what I mean. If there's something that bothers you, you can always tell me. Then it won't hurt so much.'

'What if I said why I was bad?'

'That too.' I didn't think there could be anything 'so bad' about Kerra. Maybe touching Blake's kangaroo or cowhides? I prepared myself for what she'd say, searched for encouraging comments like, *Its okay, everybody does stuff like that.* But it didn't come. She shut off, just like the generator did every night. She stuffed that thumb in her mouth and didn't even say goodnight.

I sat there, stroking wisps of her hair away from her forehead. Whether she had really gone to sleep or not, I couldn't tell, but the way she refused to talk tore at my heart. What could be so terrible that a child of ten wouldn't even say?

10

The scratches from my tumble off Rainmaker gradually healed. Mr Townsend in his no-fuss way had said I'd be fine in a week. He was right, but then he was right about most things, which was why I could never work out why he didn't intervene in Blake and Kerra's relationship. Maybe he didn't know the full extent of it.

Blake had me on Rainmaker again as soon as I could raise my leg far enough to haul myself onto the saddle. 'You have to get back on as soon as possible,' was his grinning explanation for my misery, 'or you'll lose valuable ground.' Right then I couldn't care less about catching up 'ground' with Rainmaker, or proving I was boss.

Rainmaker had just responded to my knee pressure and I was about to swing my leg over to dismount when Blake was there at my side, looking up at me. 'What do you say to a ride tomorrow? A picnic.' And before I could answer, he cut in quickly, 'Just us two.' Guess that was so I wouldn't invite Kerra. He needn't have worried as I was looking forward to time alone with him. He might talk more if we were away from the house. 'Sure,' I said.

'Sweet.' He helped me down. Apart from his closeness,

I appreciated his thoughtfulness since my back muscles still felt as if they'd been pulled to shreds.

That afternoon Blake took me in the Land Cruiser to Zack's place. He lived an hour away, across a disused railway line, in an old part of the town. 'This used to be called Ghan Town.' Blake was pumped up with 'showing me stuff'. It reminded me of when I first came to Australia last year and my friend Danny used to buy food just to show me what it was. 'There's something I think you'll appreciate, Jaime.' He steered me to a mud brick structure with a grass roof.

'This looks ancient. What is it?'

'What do you think?'

Then I saw the brass crescent and star rising above the thatch. I sucked in a breath. 'It's a mosque. In the Outback?'

Blake grinned as if he'd arranged to have it there just for me. 'It's a replica of the original one they built here when the first camel drivers came from Afghanistan in the 1860s. The local community restored it.' I watched Blake enter through the baked mud archway and, with the afternoon sun behind me, I peered in at the little circular alcove showing which direction to pray.

'Come and look inside.' Blake beckoned me, but I couldn't move. How could I have explained it? The mosque was just a monument to the past but I couldn't follow him in. I could see it all: the Afghan camel drivers washing their feet in the mosque pool, men who at the right time each day would enter the sanctuary of that mud-and-thatch and give their allegiance to the God they owed everything to. It was a men's sacred place; no women would have entered and if I had, I would have felt as if I'd trampled on a grave. It seemed different from mosques in Pakistan and it wasn't just the thatch and open walls, but my scrap of thought fled as a shout from behind brought Blake out from the mosque.

'That's Zack,' he said.

Zack's family was nothing like I expected; not like the Afghan families I knew in Adelaide. His mother had a Slim Dusty tape on and was humming to it as she bustled to the fridge and got a beer out for each boy. 'You too?' Her eyebrows asked the question of me, her hand poised in the fridge. I imagined the look on Dad's face as I toyed with accepting.

'No thanks.'

'So Zack tells me you've been to Afghanistan?'

'Yeah, early this year.'

'What's it like?' They thought they were asking normal questions and it wouldn't have bothered them if I didn't elaborate, so I don't know why I found their interest so difficult. Maybe because I'd been a captive. Also, there'd been a war going on for thirty years. I don't think I saw the best side of the country, so I had to be honest. 'It's really shot up; not so beautiful like it used to be years ago…' I paused. 'There're still untouched places and the people who have survived are rebuilding, replanting and deactivating the mines. There's even a radio station, culture being revived, music. But still fighting, everyone waiting for peace—' I was struck by how weird it seemed: me telling them what Afghanistan was like when they were the Afghans.

Just then Zack's grandmother walked in. She was the spry sort of eighty-year-old who I could imagine bungee jumping for a last fling. She looked more Afghan than any of the others, yet when she spoke her accent sounded more

Australian than mine. Her first comment confused me. 'Did you come for The Cup?'

'The Cup?' I echoed her words as if their meaning would magically come to me.

Blake helped me out. 'It was going to be a surprise. This weekend is the camel races. We're all going.'

My eyes must have shone, and Blake held my gaze longer than usual as though what he saw there was special. 'Thought you'd like that,' was all he murmured, before he turned back to the old lady. 'Nazzi, this is Jaime.'

It's an amazing feeling being introduced to a lady so old she must have the answers to life's every question. The way she was looking at me gave me the odd sensation that she knew I was still struggling with some things. I ventured a question to deflect her searching eyes from seeing further than I could myself.

'Do you remember the days when the camel drivers were here?' I wanted to ask so much more: the days of exploring, the camel strings heading north taking mail and supplies, the men in the mosque—a way of life that seemed to be lost.

'Of course. I grew up on a camel. My grandfather told me stories of Afghanistan. He was very strict. I couldn't go out of the house once I was twelve and my marriage was arranged.' Then she tipped her chin at Zack, as he lifted the can to his lips. 'No beer either. Those days are gone now.' And she sighed as though there were some things she would like to have kept. 'People knew who they were then.'

Zack's mother cut in. 'It doesn't have to stay like that. We can write it down so the young ones know.' Zack was growing restless and his grandmother put her hand over his on the table. 'Zack here, he's more Nunga than Afghan.' I thought I understood what she was trying to put into words. It was the intermarriage that had changed everything. The first Afghans who came couldn't bring their wives, so the old ways died after a few generations, their beliefs buried with them.

The atmosphere in Zack's house and what I'd seen in Nazzi's ancient, perceptive eyes stayed with me long afterwards, so that I hardly said a thing on the way home. What made a person real inside? Nazzi called herself an Afghan-Australian. How did she keep that knowledge within herself when Zack didn't show any signs of knowing?

'A penny for them?' Blake asked. Then he sighed softly. 'My mum used to say that.'

He didn't say more about his mum, so I told him what I was thinking. 'How much do you think a place influences who we are? I mean, you're different in the city.'

He shrugged. 'Living in the city, apart from study, was like a break. Here there's work—I want to be here in the Outback but, it's just—' He glanced at his side mirror.

'You'd rather fly over it,' I said, even though he was trying to say something else.

'Yeah, I guess.'

That afternoon I couldn't find Kerra; I'd checked the stable, the chook house and the garden to see if she was hiding anywhere. I started when I heard her call me from the sky. I looked up and there she was on the platform under the slowly spinning windmill blades. I shut my mouth to stop myself calling out. Wasn't that a dangerous place to be?

'Come up, Jaime.'

It took me a minute to decide to climb and when I neared the platform, she said, 'Don't stand up, Jaime, coz you're taller than me and your head might get chopped off.'

She had Sasha with her. Kerra held the cat fast until I got settled. Maybe because it was so tiny and young its middle seemed overly huge and I hoped it didn't have its kittens on the windmill platform.

'What are you doing up here?' I asked.

'Drawing the house.'

I stared out—it truly was a magnificent view. Probably like being in a low flying crop duster. Kerra laid out her pencils and gave me a sheet of paper. 'You can draw too,' she offered. We sat like that in silence for quite some time. It would be fun to learn how to do art journaling. We were so companionable that I wondered if I'd exaggerated Kerra's strangeness the night before. I looked over at her page. The house was a normal storybook one. She'd drawn the windmill too and a horse lying on the lawn. It had a leg in the air. 'Is the horse asleep?'

She shrugged. 'I don't know.'

We were quiet again while I drew a sunset over the roof of the house and a windmill black against the sky. My colouring didn't capture the sun's spectacular patterns. A breeze started up from the south and the windmill blades whirred. The woolly smell of the old shearing shed wafted into my face.

'Dad was breaking in a brumby this morning,' Kerra volunteered after a while, before I'd thought to ask about her day. 'He said it'd be a nice horse. All the others have to die.' I presumed she meant the ones they didn't catch and I tried to lift her mood.

'They do a lot of damage to the environment. They have to be killed to save the feed for the cattle and to make dogfood.'

She sighed. 'Yeah, things have to die if they don't do the right thing. Like me, I should've too.'

My hand stilled. Not for the first time I felt out of my depth with Kerra. Shouldn't she be spending time with a person trained to listen and support her? I'd mention it to Mr Townsend.

'Jaime?' I was drawing Middle Eastern designs around my page. 'I like those curvy patterns.' She pointed to the dome-like curls. 'Are they Pakistani?'

'Mmm-hmm.' I drew a minaret rising from the old shearing shed. It made me think of the fort Jasper, Liana and I were imprisoned in early this year. 'Mosques and old forts in Pakistan have arches and towers like these. In Afghanistan too—'

'What do you miss?'

'Besides people?'

'Besides Jasper, your boyfriend.' She even raised an eyebrow—I'd never heard her make a joke before.

'I told you he's not. Just a friend.' A very close friend. I blew out a breath. 'I guess I miss the high mountains, the carpet shops that smelt a bit like your shearing shed, tea shops, the aroma of curry spices, dancing in the woods at school with my friends.' With Liana mostly and I found myself smiling.

'What's funny?'

'I had a happy memory that didn't make me sad.' She nodded, seeming to understand my upside-down logic.

'I'd like a happy memory too,' she said.

I was barely listening, staring at the minaret I'd drawn. The mosque! I'd just realised what was different about the mosque in town. The sun had been behind me when I'd looked in and saw the alcove for prayer. It was facing the east. Mecca was west from here. It wasn't a true mosque at all; what Muslim would pray facing the opposite direction to Mecca? Could it have always been like that? Surely not. Had the descendants of those early camel drivers lost so much of what their ancestors believed?

I didn't feel like drawing anymore. 'I'm going to get the dinner ready. Want to see how to make lamb curry?'

Kerra packed her pencils in her Smiggles case and followed me down the ladder. I discovered how she got Sasha up there—she had a hessian shoulder bag for cat carrying. Judging by the mewling Sasha didn't care for it.

Kerra stubbornly ignored Sasha's protests and climbed down. Was she like the mosque? Something lost inside that was there once? What did she say: she wanted a happy memory? Was it painful memories that made her say and do such strange things? Or no memories at all?

11

In the morning, Blake and I saddled the horses for our picnic.

'Today I'll take you to my favourite spot,' he said as he tightened Cador's girth strap. 'I reckon you can ride that far now.'

We rode off laughing, past the dam Kerra nearly drowned in and across country in a race. We rode up a rise and I scanned the landscape sloping away behind us. We had been climbing so gradually I hadn't noticed. We reined in at the top. I gasped at the picture before me: a gorge set between two small hills.

Blake smiled and touched my hand on the reins. 'The land is so flat, so a place like this is special. It would have been a meaningful place for the Nungas too.'

I didn't let on that my legs and back still ached from my spill off Rainmaker, but this gorge was worth it. The touch of his hand too.

A tree-lined creek ran through it—no water, but I was getting used to not expecting water in creeks and rivers.

'There's a spring here but it doesn't run in the dry. And the creek fills up with a good rain,' Blake said as we walked the horses down the rise. 'It happens every now and then.' I guessed 150 millilitres of rain each year wouldn't offer many opportunities for creeks to run. A few rusty sails of a windmill rose above the bushes and as I moved Rainmaker to have a better look, a crowd of corellas soared squawking into the air.

'Since the spring was unreliable, they dug a well here ages ago. The windmill pumped the water up for the horses. It used to be a changeover station for Cobb and Co.' We looped the horses' reins over the branch of a tree that had three different trunks growing from the main butt. The mulga trees were everywhere. 'We also have a lot of desert oaks and those are river red gums by the creek.' I looked around me. A place like that, with a sense of history, always got to me: what would the people who'd lived here say if they could see us now?

Blake led me to the ruins of a single-roomed house. The heart of it still stood: a single fireplace, bare against the spindly grass, and a solitary trough—they bore witness to a land Europeans didn't understand. We sat under a silver eucalyptus tree, its bark velvety, and looking as though it'd been there since the creek first carved itself into the land.

Blake made himself busy pulling a small frypan and billy from his saddle bag. He had a faint smile on his face as if he was counting his blessings and was pleased with how many he had. Then, after he got the fire going and the damper cooked to his liking, he held out his hands to the food and nodded at me to tuck in. He was so happy. I was just thinking how Kerra would enjoy a picnic when Blake floored me.

'Thanks for what you're doing with Kerra.' I never expected him to bring up the subject of his sister by himself.

'With Kerra?' It sounded as if she was the furthermost thing from my mind, which wasn't true.

'Yeah. She's been a lot better lately.'

'What do you mean?' I hoped I'd hear his side of the story at last.

'You've kept her occupied. She's doing her jobs, caught up on her school work. Matt says she's really taken to you.'

'So she's keeping out of trouble.'

Maybe my tone was sharp because Blake gave me a quick glance.

'Can I ask you something, Blake?'

He made a sound which I took to mean 'sure'. I should have noticed how defensive he sounded. 'Why do you discipline Kerra? She's just your sister.' I was calm and wasn't ready for the way he spat out the answer as though it was warm beer.

'She's a little witch!' A slap in the face wouldn't have made me flinch more. 'Dad doesn't see it all. He's busy. It's better for me to get it over and done with. If Mum was here, she'd—'

He stopped suddenly and before I could show that I wanted to understand, he leaned over and offered me an empty mug. 'Let's just enjoy this here, hey?'

But I couldn't let it rest. He sounded frustrated so how could he stop talking? 'You don't have to feel like you've got to fill your mum's shoes. I wouldn't like a brother doing that to me.'

He stayed silent as if he was thinking about it. When he finally spoke it was like I'd never spoken at all. 'When you swing the billy like this it makes the tea taste better.' And there he was, standing with the billy swinging round his head, showing me as if that had been my question.

With Kerra I'd learnt to wait, let her answer in her own

good time. I was used to people beating round the bush—my Pakistani friends did that a lot. But I knew it was politeness with them. This was as though Blake shut the door because he was in pain, trying to keep control before he lost it.

It shocked me to see what my questions had stirred up. I tried to apologise. 'Blake—'

'Look, Jaime! We came out here for a picnic. So let's just have a picnic. Is that too much to ask?'

'I'm sorry, I didn't mean—'

He turned to face me. 'You don't understand.' He said it slowly, as if he was trying to restrain how he spoke and I wished he didn't have to do that. Sure, I didn't understand, but I didn't want him to be so upset. Now I had no idea how to fix it, how to get him to be the happy Blake who brought me there.

'When Mum died Kerra had to be taken in hand. That's all there is to it.' He said 'died' with his voice so tight that I fully expected him to lean right over and tell me to get out of his face. But he didn't, just threw the billy of tea on the fire and shoved things into his saddle bag. 'If you think Dad should have spent more time with her—'

'I wasn't—' Worse and worse. The fire sizzled and died.

'—it doesn't work like that on a property like this.'

I chewed the inside of my cheek, watching him by his horse now, the energy in him making his legs shift, his hands restless, on his hips, in the air, making me wish I could turn back the clock.

'When jobs need doing here, you have to do them—fencing, bringing cattle in. When the shearers come, you shear. When it doesn't rain, you check the bores. Nothing stops for a ten-year-old. Kids have to pull their weight, ride with it. I did.'

Kerra might be different but I didn't dare say so. I knew when enough was enough. He was waiting by his horse, the buckles on his saddle bag done up and I wasn't sure what to do. Should I say let's go? Say I was sorry again? Guess I'd started it but right then, I thought an apology would be like throwing pearls to the swine.

His saddle crackled as he mounted and he turned Cador to look at me. 'Well? Are you coming or should I tell Kerra to come and get you?' That stung and I found my tongue again as I stood up.

'Sure, and you don't need to talk to me like this.'

He didn't answer that, just brought Cador near to Rainmaker, and then leaned down so I could feel the heat of his breath on my face.

'Kerra has to be kept an eye on or she could do something…weird. You'll see.' He said 'weird' as though it wasn't the word he wanted to use, as if the truth would be too shocking.

What on earth could he mean? And I couldn't ask, not with his I-only-wanted-a-picnic frown. I followed him home, all the time mulling over how I could cope with him like this. No wonder he never spoke about Kerra in Adelaide. No wonder he was different, happy there; *she* hadn't been there. There had to be some way of sorting all the feelings—his and mine—but right then I'd had what he'd call 'a gutful'. I felt like Pandora opening the box: too much to handle and too late to put it all back.

Later on I was out feeding the chooks when Matt and Richelle drove up with mail for Mr Townsend. Richelle made a beeline for the stables to find Blake, but Matt called to me.

I'd had enough of guys for one day and only waved, but he strolled over before they left.

'G'day.' He said that as if he was The Man from Snowy River and I let a grin slip. Matt certainly had raw charm. 'What's up?'

'Why should anything be up?' I forgot how observant he was. Could he tell I'd been crying? He didn't answer, just stood there and waited. I knew he wouldn't go until I told him. 'Just had a spot of trouble with Blake, that's all.'

He seemed to tense slightly, but I may have imagined it since his tone was slow and careless as he asked, 'What sort of trouble?'

'Just an argument. I asked something I shouldn't have.'

He relaxed then, leaning against the gate as if he was floating on air—but if I kicked the gate, he'd fall for sure.

'Uh-huh,' was all he said at first, then, 'What'd ya say?'

'It was about Kerra. He just blew up. One minute he was happy, the next it was like being on a Pacific island with a volcano erupting.' I thought for a bit longer, thankful that Matt didn't butt in. 'Now I'm not sure what to do—whether we've lost ground. I mean, I'm not sure now if we had any in the first place.'

The toe of Matt's boot made a slow pattern in the dust. 'I wouldn't worry,' he said finally, as if the marks on the ground had given him the answer. 'Just let him go. It'll blow over and you'll be able to talk sense then.'

With Matt I had to read between the lines. I hoped I

didn't take too much license whenever I did, as I desperately wanted Blake to get over whatever it was that bothered him about Kerra. Matt didn't stay long after that, just squeezed my shoulder like my brother Andrew might have done and made his way back to his ute and dogs. When he started the engine, Richelle appeared. I didn't imagine it, she glowered at me as if she wished me dead.

I was in the kitchen when Blake came in. I knew it was him by his step and the way he was standing there, probably watching me.

'Jaime.'

I turned round, hoping the blotches on my face had cleared up. 'About today—' He hung his hat on the hook by the door and came closer. 'I didn't mean to flip out like that. I just wanted us to have a nice time. I'm sorry.'

Mum had always told me to accept an apology in grace and I fought down the impulse to ask him another question while he was receptive. 'That's cool. I'm sorry too. Just trying to help, I guess.' I had to be careful as to even imply he needed help might start the sparks flying again.

He put an arm round me and hugged me, making me shrug the thoughts of Kerra aside. Surely it was just a case of a big brother trying to do his best for his little sister? He was still Blake. Couldn't I like him, warts and all? Who was perfect anyway? Certainly not me.

By late afternoon I was missing Kerra. I thought she would have been around to meet me after the picnic but she didn't seem to be near the house. I guessed she'd be with her father but when he came in for his afternoon smoko he hadn't seen her either. 'She's often down at the dam,' he offered when I asked. 'I've seen her there with Bow when he's free.'

Cooking the tea could wait; this was the longest she'd gone without showing up. I had to find her, as urgently as a voice in my mind telling me to hurry up. I rushed out to the dam.

At first I didn't see her. Bow was sitting at the dam's edge but he was subdued, his nose on his paws. Funny how dogs seem to pick up on our moods. He licked my hand though, when I patted him. 'Where's Kerra?' He lifted his head, then I heard the sobs.

She was on the other side, crouched over. I walked round to her, wondering what to say. She had a cardboard box. The sobs were relentless: not of a child, rather an adult wishing they could die. Suddenly I could see what she was doing.

'No! Kerra.' I broke into a run. 'Kerra!' I had to stop her. And when I reached her I hauled her back, pulled her hands out of the water. 'Don't do that.' I was sobbing too by then, and I prised open her fingers and checked the wet, matted fur. My eyes travelled from the tiny wet body in the mud to the one in her hands. There was nothing else I could say. There was no malice in her eyes—no evil—just pain, and a sadness that a child shouldn't feel.

'Why?' All sorts of possibilities ran through my head. Surely Blake wouldn't have found the kittens already and made her drown them herself? I couldn't believe he would be that cruel. I held her close to me while I unclenched her fingers again and put the kitten down with the other one. It was still warm under the wet fur, but its little head hung limply. She saw it as I laid it down, and the sobs started up again; mine too. I'd never found anyone killing an animal with no reason. I didn't know what to say.

Then she tried to talk. I heard the first part. It sounded like 'I had to.' I sat her back a bit from me as I tried to make sense out of it.

'What do you mean, "you had to"?' But she wouldn't say anything else. I sensed if she didn't talk about this to me, it would be another thing she'd store up to haunt herself with, and who knew how much stuff she already had in there.

'Kerra, tell me. I will understand. What happened today?'

It seemed she wasn't going to tell, but then she wiped one arm across her face.

'Sasha was having her kittens...' She drew in a breath. 'One came out, then Sasha started yowling. When another one was coming, Sasha was running round the shed. The kitten was stuck and dragging on the ground and Sasha still ran all over the place, howling. I didn't know what to do. Then Sasha sat down, but the same thing happened for the last one. It doesn't go like that with the cats in the shed. They just have their kittens quiet, only growl once or twice, not howl and run. Her eyes were scared, Jaime. The kittens killed her.'

'She's dead?' Surely she was exaggerating, but she gave a slow nod. Then she turned to me, the brown tear stains on her face making her look macabre, but I pushed that thought aside.

'Jaime, they had to die, don't you see? They were bad. They killed their mother.' The sobs started again. 'I loved Sasha and they killed her. I'm bad too.' I guessed she meant she was bad for killing the kittens, but I had to get her to see it wasn't the kittens' fault.

'Kerra, it was an accident. Things like that happen. It was no one's fault. Sasha was too little, that's all.'

'They killed her,' she whispered. Suddenly a thought struck me. Hadn't she mentioned three kittens? Carefully I looked over her head into the box and, sure enough, there was a dry ball of fur. So I'd been quick enough to save it, but wouldn't she feel she had to drown it too? I had to make sure before I reminded her of it.

'Kerra...' I hesitated. 'Do you want to be brave, like Gul in Begal's polo story?'

I felt her nod, but then I heard her whisper, 'I can't be brave. I'm not strong like Gul.'

'Brave means you do something when it's very hard to do. If you were strong and it was easy to do, it wouldn't be brave.'

She sniffed. 'What's brave now?'

I spoke slowly, hoping she wouldn't react. 'The bravest thing now is to let the last kitten off the hook. It wasn't his fault.'

She twisted in my arms to stare into the box. My heart sank. I could imagine her thinking, 'oh, I missed one', and *zap*, it would be in the dam too. Her hand reached out and I watched as it hovered over the kitten. I was ready to pounce, not wanting to witness more death.

She let her hand drop and settled back in my arms, one dirty thumb in her mouth. She pulled it out a moment to speak. 'You take it,' was all she said. She didn't say another word. I wasn't sure what I expected: remorse, an admission of wrong? An 'Oh, I'm sorry' such as Elly would have said? But I couldn't imagine Elly doing any of what happened that day.

One small thing comforted me: Kerra didn't try to destroy the last kitten. Surely that was progress. I told her

I was proud of her saving it. Reminding her of the others wasn't going to help.

The sky was dark purple by the time we headed for the house to bury Sasha and the two kittens in the garden. I carried the box. Bow led the way.

12

Feeding a kitten with a tiny eye dropper was not as much fun as it looked. It was like getting white pinballs into the clowns' mouths at the show, with no hope of a prize at the end. I was just wishing I had three hands when Kerra arrived. She said nothing, just watched, not offering to help. I dared not ask for any as I didn't want to push her, so it stunned me when I finally realised why she'd come.

'Leave that.' She sounded like Blake when he spoke to her.

'Why?'

'You don't need to feed it. I have a better idea.'

This I had to see. 'Okay.'

She stretched out her hand for the kitten. I hoped she didn't notice the way I tensed as she picked it up, nor how much of an effort it was not to offer to carry it. She held the kitten carefully though, and I followed her out, down the hall, through the back door, past Blake's room. It was dark outside, the hum of the generator making me think of a monster purring for its dinner.

'Where're we going?'

'The shed.' To the scene of the original crime. What

did she have in mind? My fertile imagination thought of numerous possibilities, none of which I liked. Then Bow was padding beside us and nothing seemed bizarre anymore. Bow reminded me of Matt; made me feel secure in my ability to cope with whatever Kerra dished up.

'See?' Inside she stretched up and flicked a switch to cast light on half the shed. She pointed to the ceiling. I followed the direction of her finger. The hayloft? 'We have to go up there,' came her quiet voice and, shifting the kitten into one hand, she started up the steel ladder. The kitten mewed weakly.

'You sure you can manage, Kerra? Do you want me to take the kitten?'

But she didn't answer, even though she must have heard. I didn't care much for the ladder; it was long and bowed in the middle. The shed was high and business-like, nothing like the comfortable barns in movies.

Up there it was difficult to see as the tube-light was below us, but I crawled behind Kerra through the hay, hoping I wasn't disturbing rats or snakes.

She stopped. 'There.'

I peered over her shoulder and began to crawl closer. 'Don't,' was all she whispered. Then, as if she knew she'd sounded bossy, she explained. 'She's wild, Jaime. She doesn't know you. She might run.' Kerra leaned over slowly, all the while murmuring in a sing-song type of mew as she gently put the kitten close to a feral cat. 'She's got kittens herself. See, Jaime?'

I held my breath, waiting to see if the farm cat would accept Sasha's kitten as her own. We must have sat there for five minutes, saying nothing, just watching. She didn't eat it, which seemed a good sign. She sniffed it all over, then began licking it. Kerra backed up through the hay.

'C'mon, Jaime.'

'Will it be okay?' I was thinking how I'd know the difference between my kittens and a ring-in if I were feline, but I was floored by Kerra's childlike faith in mother cats. 'She can't count. The kitten'll be fine.'

'How come she doesn't run from you?'

'I'm up here heaps. She knows my smell.' So that's why Kerra had to carry the kitten.

Getting down the ladder was a bit of a worry. Kerra waited for me at the bottom without hurrying me like usual.

'Would Liana have given the kitten to another cat?' she asked as we returned to my room.

'Kerra, the most important thing is that *you* did. It was a special thing to do.'

'But would've she?'

Kerra was in stubborn mode again and it was hard to shift her, so since I didn't think it would matter, I said, 'Sure. Liana liked animals. She was kind.'

'And she was brave.'

I sighed. 'Yes. She grew brave.'

'Tell me more about her and Mr Kimberley. How he pretended to be her brother.' She didn't hide the yearning in her tone: that wanting to be Liana's brother so badly showed his care. Even that first day I had seen that Blake didn't have those feelings for his little sister, so I was encouraged that she'd mentioned Mr Kimberley. So far I'd thought the idea of an almost perfect brother was too far beyond her experience and understanding for her to accept. But I wanted her to see there was another way to live, and she could choose to have it.

Kerra settled herself on my bed, subdued but waiting. The absence of Sasha lay heavy between us and all I felt like doing was picking Kerra up and hugging her, but she didn't have a *hug me* look on her face. I was learning her different facial expressions: the blank one she kept for Blake. Right now, I could tell she had a lot on her mind, but I knew she wouldn't discuss it. She glanced at me. I wasn't sure how much of 'a good brother' she'd be able to stand, so instead of telling Liana and Mr Kimberley's adventure, I plunged in with one of Elly's favourite folktales.

'This is called "The Mysterious Traveller".' Kerra sighed. It was the relief of a weary traveller finally finding rest. 'It's a beautiful story from Elly's favourite storybook.' I told the tale of an old desert guide called Issa, who found a lost baby after a dust storm. Around the child's neck was a gold pendant shaped like a half-star. No one knew who she was, so Issa took her home and named her Mariama.' Kirra touched her half-ring.

'Did he adopt her?'

I nodded. 'As she grew she also learned how to guide people through the desert. When she was almost grown Issa became blind. "This is why God gave me to you, Baba," she said, "to be your eyes."

'One day a young man and his aide arrived needing a guide, but when they realised Issa was blind, they set off by themselves. Issa and Mariama followed their tracks to check on them, when a huge storm blew up.'

Kirra's thumb popped out. 'They saved the men?'

'Yes, and the young man returned to Issa's house to thank them. That was when he noticed the pendant around Mariama's neck. "Where did you find that?"

"'I've always had it, since my grandfather found me."

'Hope sprang in to the young man's eyes. "'What do you mean?"

'Issa told him the story of a lost baby in the desert. "Who are you?" he asked when he had finished.

"'My name is Abbas," said the young man. "My father is the king of Sana and when I was young, we were attacked. I was taken to my eldest uncle and my baby sister was sent to another uncle, but she never arrived. We have been looking for her all this time." He stared at Mariama.

"'How would you know her," Issa said slowly.

'Abbas pulled a pendant out from his robe. "She will have the other half of this." He stretched his open hand to Mariama and she took off her pendant to lay it in his palm. The pendants formed an eight-pointed star. Abbas showed Mariama some marks in the gold. "These words say: The Children of Sana. Salaam, my sister." His voice cracked. "Will you love me?"

'She nodded and he wrapped his arms around her. Then she said, "But I cannot leave my grandfather. He needs me."

"'Sire," Abbas said to Issa. "Please come and live in our palace. We will become one family."

'Mariama put her hand on Issa's shoulder. "I will still be your eyes, Baba."

'Abbas said, "And together we will heal my father's heart."'

Kerra was warm and floppy in my quilt. I didn't have the heart to send her back to her own room. She didn't comment on the story so I let her rest and checked emails on my iPhone. One from Mum. She mentioned Kerra and hoped she was getting on fine. *So hard for a young child to lose a parent.*

Of course I hadn't told Mum about Blake's reactions to Kerra. That would have worried Dad; he might have even travelled up to check Blake out or asked me to come home. Maybe I should have told Mum about the kittens but I felt a loyalty to the Townsends. I just hoped I wouldn't regret it. Another email from Jasper to read later. One from Dad checking in to see if I was okay. I sighed. Our family seemed so uncomplicated in comparison to the Townsends. I glanced at Kerra. I was hoping she would see love as a two-way street, but I knew she wouldn't take to anything that she hadn't thought out for herself.

When she finally spoke, I realised she was sharper than I thought. The thumb came out first.

'Mariama decided to love the prince?'

I nodded again.

'Can you choose stuff like that? Did you choose to like Blake?'

'Sort of. Most people would disagree, but my friend Liana believed that you can choose to love a person.'

'So can it go the other way? If you don't love someone at all, you can choose to love them?'

I bit my lip. I felt like hugging her fiercely and dancing her round the room, but I knew she wouldn't appreciate my emotion.

'Yes.' And I gathered her to me gently, feeling like a scientist who'd made a brilliant breakthrough in her research.

I wasn't ready for the next progression in her thinking; I

was counting on her response, not her brother's.

'Jaime? Do you think Blake could ever love me like that?'

I stared at her and said the only thing I could think of. 'Could you love him?'

She fell quiet and in that silence I realised I had been wrong about her feelings for Blake. She didn't hate him at all.

13

The next day I needed to talk with Mr Townsend. The world seemed quieter than usual, eerie, as if a celestial being like the sun had ceased to function. Kerra snuck into my room while I was dressing and, in her usual way, acted strangely. Her behaviour wouldn't have been strange for another child, which made it even more disturbing. She picked up the photo of her mother—she'd never shown any interest in it before—and said flatly, 'This is my mother.'

'I know.' I did up my shirt buttons.

'She's beautiful, isn't she?' She said it as though it was the first time she'd ever noticed.

I knelt by her. 'That's where you and Blake get all your good looks.' She didn't smile at my efforts to lighten up her mood, so I tried a different tack to get her talking. 'Your mum looks kind and happy.'

'I don't know. She looks it, but I don't remember.' There was nothing else to say, nothing I could help her with. I had to get some answers. Blake wasn't ready to talk. Besides, I kept making a botch of all our conversations; it was as if Kerra was driving a wedge between us. Matt was leaving it to the family and that meant Mr Townsend. If I'd asked Mum she would have said he was the first 'port of call'.

I found Mr Townsend after lunch at the windmill, a spanner in hand, a toolbox close by.

'What's the matter with it?' That's what was missing in the morning: the clanking of the pump as it let the water flow up into the tank.

'Nothing that a few bangs with a spanner won't fix.' He stood up. He was making light of it; he wasn't one to explain every single detail. Like Matt. And Blake. I blew out a quiet breath. This wouldn't be easy.

'Where does the water come from?'

'The dam.' He indicated vaguely the direction of the dam nearest the house. 'If we don't get rain soon we'll have to sink another bore. Expensive business that.'

He bent to do something to the pump and I wasn't sure how to get his attention again, to steer the conversation onto his wife. As it happened, he opened the way himself. 'Kerra says you tell her stories.' He spoke as he worked, head down.

'Yes, at night usually, before she goes to bed.'

'She says you're quite an actor.' He banged the spanner again. 'She seems more settled, happier.' So he did notice what went on about him. 'Kerra's been through a lot, poor kid.' He stopped what he was doing and looked up. 'S'pose I should've married again, given her another mother-figure, but single women fall out of the sky even less frequently than the rain in these parts.'

I smiled politely. I wanted to ask what Kerra had been through, but I asked about her mother instead. Matt was probably right about it being related to her. 'Mr Townsend, did Kerra's mother die in childbirth?'

He stood up then, wiping his hands on his faded jeans. At first I didn't think he would answer as he bent down again, putting tools in the box, one by one, as though I wasn't there. I wasn't sure if I was being ignored or the thought process was taking longer than usual.

'That pump should be all right now. Should probably ditch it for solar panels.'

The pump? Was I meant to make conversation about the *pump*? He still hadn't looked at me since I'd asked about his wife and my mind was lost on how to turn the conversation back to Mrs Townsend when he spoke again.

'No, lass, she didn't.' The look on his face made me wish I hadn't asked about his wife at all, but I stuck it out for Kerra'a sake.

'Kerra doesn't remember anything about her and I think it would help her to know.'

'Do you now.' He regarded me for a few moments, making me feel like a meddling fool.

I kept babbling on. 'I really think that she needs to talk to someone. I have a sister much the same age. Kerra seems a little...' I couldn't decide how to put it and was surprised when he supplied the words.

'Mixed up?'

I almost nodded but stopped myself in time. 'Not totally. I mean, she's clever and seems a lot older in some ways, but it worries me how she thinks she's so bad.'

If I didn't have his undivided attention before, I did now.

'She said that?'

'Often. She says Blake thinks so too.

'Anyone else?'

'No. Only Blake. And I don't understand.' I could see why Blake could get annoyed with her at times; she wasn't the model child, but I thought I saw more than he did, from spending time with her and telling stories. I saw the façade, the blank and stubborn barrier hiding a frightened and confused little girl. I could even understand the responsibility he felt towards her; I'd feel the same if it were Elly. It was just the lack of kindness and care I found hard to fathom—he showed those things to me and everyone else. What made Kerra different?

Mr Townsend led me over to the fence, where he leaned against a post and began taking out tobacco and a paper. I thought something was coming; a man like him didn't make a rollie for nothing when he had work to do. Maybe it gave him time to think, get his thoughts in order, and I tried not to show my impatience. I was more hopeful after he finally lit it. But if I thought he was going to tell me anything, 'I had another thing coming' as I'd heard him say to Blake at times.

He'd forgotten I was there and I realised he wouldn't say anything at all—his grief was still raw and I wondered if that's what made him seem quiet and only 'half there' at times. I left him leaning against the fence, one leg on the bottom wire, his hat turned down, with his shadowy thoughts for company.

When Kerra came in to the kitchen that afternoon with her drawing book, she seemed different. At first I couldn't put my finger on what it was. It made me wonder if Mr Townsend had spoken to her. I burned with wanting to know what had happened all those years ago. Wouldn't it be easier for them to talk about it? I was making Moroccan pizza with the bases I'd found in the huge freezer and the inevitable lamb.

Kerra wasn't helping but drawing a picture of her and her dad holding hands. There was a gap and then Blake. She drew him bigger than her dad. Was that because he was important to her or because he was scary?

'Was Princess Noori in the Prince Hamid story beautiful?' she asked while she looked for a colour in her pencil case.

'The narrator says so. Though it's inside beauty that's important,' I added, remembering Mum's pep talks.

She spoke while she coloured the sky purple. 'Dad told me what a beautiful person Mum was and how she named me. Tamsyn is my second name because it means "Thomas" and that was her family name. And she named me Kerra because it means "dearer" in Cornish. And "beloved".' How clever of Mr Townsend. 'Dad said how she used to hug me and love me.'

Then her expression changed, and I caught the whispered words, 'But that was before.'

I stiffened as a familiar feeling crept over me: there was something scary in Kerra's thoughts and I wasn't sure how to handle it.

'You know how bad, I was?'

I shook my head, willing myself to stay calm. This was just a sad and frightened little girl. 'No, tell me.' *It's always best to tell*, Mum's voice resounded in my head.

She hesitated. 'You'll still like me?'

'Absolutely.' I held my breath even though I thought of numerous things it could be, but there were still shocks in store for me.

'I ruined Blake's life.'

'No!' That wasn't what I expected. 'That's not true.' She was only a child. How could she ruin someone's life, or even think she did?

'Dad said it wasn't my fault that Mum died, but he wasn't there, he doesn't know. It was.'

'Who said it was your fault?' I couldn't stay calm anymore or keep my voice steady. 'Who said? Kerra, who!' But I forgot she was used to people bigger than her telling her loudly what to do. She pulled her firm blank face down, the one she kept for Blake.

If she knew, she wasn't going to tell.

Later, Blake was teaching me to dance in the kitchen in preparation for The Cup. I should have been chopping red onions for the pizzas. Matt had rung saying he and Richelle would pop in to watch footy with us, so Blake said he'd cook the pizzas outside. The Townsends had a brick pizza oven in the garden that Blake and his dad had built when he was younger.

'Most of the guys know all the dances, so you don't have to worry much.'

'What do you mean "most of the guys"?'

'Well, in half the dances you change partners, like this barn dance I'm trying to show you if you'd put that knife down. They still have a lot of the old dances at these shindigs because everybody goes, even kids. Though lately they all end up line dancing, especially at a do like The Cup when it's outside.'

Then I wanted to know how to line dance. When Blake was like that—laughing and chuckling and purposely tripping me up so I'll fall into his arms—I could forget that Kerra's problems loomed between us. He made me only think of the Camel Cup and how much fun we'd have in the night, dancing on the race track. The best country band in the state had been hired and in the excitement, I forgot my earlier resolve to keep Kerra out of our conversations.

'Kerra will go?'

'Yep.' And I felt a definite drawing back when I mentioned her name. That was my time for keeping quiet. I was learning not to give into that urge to 'interfere' as Blake called it. To me it was 'being helpful'.

'Blake, I tried to talk with your father yesterday. About your mother.'

'He told me.' I thought he'd say more and I waited before I asked the next bit; I didn't want a repeat of the scene at the gorge.

'What was it like when she died?'

He shrugged. 'I got through it. It was hard. Mum and I had a special relationship. We were much alike.' He seemed cool but there was a mixture of hurt and sadness in his eyes. I'd seen that in Kerra's face at times and I stepped forward quickly and hugged him. I'd learnt something the other day: don't get in a guy's face when he's talking about his feelings.

When I pulled away he said softly, 'Let's get up early tomorrow. I'll take you on a road trip in the Cruiser. Tons of things to show you.'

He pulled me closer to him again and I laid my head against his chest. I breathed in the smell of him, the hint of deodorant underlying the horse scent I was growing to enjoy. Mum's voice was in my head, *more time together always helps relationships*.

'Sure,' I said.

My emotions were buoyant when Matt and Richelle arrived. It was always a treat to see Matt, and Richelle even complimented both Blake and me on the pizzas. That night there was no reception to watch the footy, so we stood around the oven, keeping warm while listening to a battery radio—not that I understood much. Dad had tried to teach me introductory AFL but it hadn't stuck. At least I knew the two South Australian teams. I caught Richelle's glance shifting from me to Blake a few times, but I tried not to let anything bother me. She didn't glower at me for once, even when Blake put his arm around me. Then I realised, if Blake was happy, so was Richelle.

14

We left at six in the ute. It was still dark. Blake had packed a thermos of tea and lamb-and-beetroot sandwiches. I didn't say how over lamb I was. He had poured milk in the tea and it reminded me of Pakistani chai. Chai always accompanied fellowship and I looked forward to the day ahead as if I were on an excursion to the Karakorum Mountains.

'You don't mind coming in the ute?' he asked. 'I only use the Mazda for driving down to Adelaide.'

I shook my head, remembering the old blue car he had in Adelaide. Blake put a CD on.

'Sorry I don't have a place to plug an iPod in.' His taste in music was eclectic: John Mayer to Guy Sebastian, as well as old stuff like U2 and the Bee Gees. Even country.

'You don't like heavy music?' Kate Sample said country music was just for hicks from the bush.

He shook his head. 'Too much in my head already without compounding it.'

People were always surprising. Take me: I missed out on a decade of Western music growing up in Pakistan, so I liked classics, Celtic, even Keith Urban. I kept that pretty quiet, as I suspected this was a music map of my mother's generation.

'Keep an eye out for roos and emus,' Blake said. We'd just passed a sign about wandering stock as well. 'Sunrise and dusk are the worst time for roos, but emus are so dumb they cross the road at any time.'

It took an hour to town and another on the Oodnadatta track to reach Farina.

'I want you to see this,' Blake said with a mysterious smile. He sounded like Danny had last year wanting to show me a movie theatre. 'This' was a ghost town that was in the process of being restored. 'Volunteers come during July to work on it,' he said. 'Too hot any other time.'

We walked down lanes where a bank, shops, a school and houses had once stood. There were ruins of some, just the foundations or underground storerooms of others. I looked through an ancient window at the spinifex-littered desert, stretching to the horizon below a bright blue sky. I imagined living here in the nineteenth century: washing clothes by hand, cooking in a wood oven, writing endless letters and waiting for camel strings to bring supplies and the mail.

Blake stepped behind me and, just then, my stomach gurgled. We hadn't had much breakfast, just dried fruit. He chuckled.

'This isn't all, there's a huge baker's oven.' He took me across the dirt road to see it. It had been restored. 'The oldest working oven in Australia,' Blake said with pride. 'Bakers from all over the country come to volunteer to run the bakery during the winter.'

It was underground. I stepped down to look at the black-and-gold metal work. A huge wooden spatula, like a pizza ladle, stood to the side. I'd seen an old oven like this in Pakistan; it was used for baking naan.

I could smell delicious yeasty things. 'Do we get to sample the bread?'

Blake grabbed my hand. 'We get to have breakfast.'

We walked hand in hand towards a tent where the baked goods were sold. My hand felt warm in his and I knew it was going to be a great day.

'Choose,' he said.

I opted for an egg-and-bacon roll and a finger bun. Blake also bought old-fashioned loaves to take home.

'It will be shut on the way back,' he explained.

I took pics to put on Facebook later for my family. Maybe Jasper and Ayesha would see them too. Elly would love a giant oven; she was already showing a talent with food. Blake took a selfie of us. We laughed so hard, but we looked good in twin Akubras—his blond hair sticking out under the brim and my plait slung over my shoulder.

On the two-hour trip to Beltana, I thought how different Blake was away from the homestead. Like stones slid off his shoulders. He was full of jokes and stories from the flying school he attended north of Adelaide. Nothing about when he was young though. At that moment a ute flew past us in a cloud of dust from the opposite direction, then I saw the emus.

'Look!'

Blake slowed down but the emus couldn't decide which way to go. One strutted across and stopped halfway, thought better of it and ran back, only to try again.

'See what I mean?' Blake said.

He kept the ute rolling slowly and finally we got through without hitting any of those long legs. I looked back and yelled for Blake to stop.

'What's wrong?'

'There's another emu there in the bush on the other side of the road. It can't get up.' I stared in horror as the bird continually flapped to rise but flopped back to the ground. Blake stopped the ute.

'It's been hit.' He said more under his breath that I didn't catch. He strode to the back of the ute. I jumped out and saw him load his rifle.

'What are you doing? Isn't there an animal rescue group up here?'

Blake put the gun down and came to me, putting his hands gently on my shoulders.

'Jaime, its legs are broken. Like a horse, it won't survive. Can't eat in the wild without legs.'

He picked the gun up and strode over to the bird. I didn't look, just got into the ute. There was only one shot. I had tears in my eyes. When Blake started the engine again, he laid a hand on mine.

'Dingoes or eagles would have ripped it apart. This way it won't suffer.'

We were quiet after that, me staring down the straight gravel road, thinking about the harsh reality of living up there. Blake gave no indication of what he was thinking.

Then, right out of the blue, he asked, 'Were there places like this in Pakistan?' Lately he'd hardly mentioned my former life and it startled me.

'Um, yeah, down south there is desert, in the Sindh. But I didn't go there, just passed through once on a train trip to Karachi.'

'You've seen a lot.'

'Guess so. Coming home for holidays we stayed in Singapore, Malaysia, even the Philippines once, just for a few days.'

'Do you like living here more or do you have a hankering to go back?'

I glanced at him, but he faced the road ahead, a muscle clenching in his cheek.

'Australia has a higher standard of living than Third World countries like Pakistan, but there'll always be things I miss. Almost my whole childhood was spent there. I miss special places and atmosphere—but I'm feeling an atmosphere up here too.'

He smiled then. 'Yep, life's better up here than in the city. I could get bored down there.'

I wondered, if it was so much better up here, why he couldn't be happy at home. I realised that it wasn't the Outback or isolation which bothered him. It had to be Kerra and I wished I knew why.

We reached Beltana by lunchtime and Blake straightaway took me to the museum in the shearing shed.

'This is where Afghan camel drivers bred camels. Explorers would come to choose them for their expeditions. Ernest Giles took camels from here to find a way across the desert to Perth. He was the first European to do it.'

'So where are the camels?' I asked.

'None here anymore. They were let go when the trucks took over their carting business. Now we have half a million in the wild. We ship a few to Saudi for racing or eating, but not as many as people think.'

In the museum I soaked up the history of the Afghans

and their camels who came to SA. I touched camel bags, similar to some I'd seen in Pakistan, even a shalwar qameez and a man's woollen shawl. There were old rugs too. When we emerged I saw three alpacas stalking across the yard as though they were dogs on patrol. I chuckled; no camels, just alpacas.

We drove to a secluded spot—not hard to do in the far north—where there was a well and a canal.

'They call this an Afghan well, where they used to water the camels.' A round tank made of stones stood nearby. 'Stockmen use it now.' Blake had a picnic rug and laid out the plastic boxes of sandwiches and two tin cups for the tea. We sat side by side.

He spread his hands apart as if offering a feast. 'Dig in,' he said.

I took a sandwich and eyed it warily. Even warm lamb with gravy was wearing thin. Surprisingly I liked the cold lamb and beetroot combination.

'Tastier than you'd expect,' I said.

'Yep.'

Blake was a nice guy and I wondered if his treatment of Kerra was born of some sort of hurt. I poured us a cup of tea each. It was still hot. I sighed. A bird called, then another; the sun was shining.

'It's lovely out here.'

'Jaime—'

In his outstretched hand was a stone. I took it. 'It's a heart. Where did you find it?'

He pointed to the ground. 'Just here. Mum used to find them everywhere. One time she went to the beach on Yorke

Peninsula to see a friend and came back with one for each of us.'

He was staring at me, the green in his eyes darkening like deep water. My breath caught as he leaned closer. As our lips touched, his hand cradled my head. His mouth was warm, so gentle, and it felt as though our hearts were opening, fusing, like the night we watched the stars, only sweeter. He sat back.

'I've wanted to do that for a while.'

I breathed in to steady myself.

'Maybe we should do it again then.'

We returned late (we'd spent a long time just lying side by side, describing what shapes the wispy clouds turned into) but I still found Kerra awake in my room. She seemed less strange; the talk with her dad must have helped. Or maybe it was just me, seeing her through different eyes.

'I want to do something special like Mariama.' Her face shone, the first time I'd seen it like that. She looked almost like Elly and any other ten-year-old. I scooped her up in my arms. 'I could save Blake.'

I still had my arms around her, but I stiffened and slowly released her. 'You've already done something special. Remember how you let the kitten off the hook? That was brave.'

'That kitten's all right now.' Then I saw a touch of the old Kerra again. 'I wish someone would save me like the kitten. Like Mr Kimberley and Liana saved you.'

That could be a normal childish reaction to a story like Liana's, but I knew there was more, and I took a punt: 'Do you believe me when I say that you are not to blame for your mum's death, Kerra. It happened; it was no one's fault.' I don't think she heard me.

'Do you think God's real, Jaime?'

'Sure I do. And I reckon He doesn't blame you. Your dad doesn't blame you, Blake doesn't either.' I hoped I was right about that last one.

Kerra's face brightened for a moment, then it clouded over.

'Blake does so.'

'How do you know? Just because he's not kind to you?' My fingers closed around the stone in my pocket.

'No.'

'Shouts sometimes?' I tried to humour her out of the mood I could tell was looming.

'He only shouts when I annoy him on purpose.'

'How then?' And I felt the fear choking me, telling me to stop asking, to change the subject. *Jaime, you won't want to know.*

'He told me.'

At first I was silent, and my voice was deathly quiet when I continued questioning her. I had to keep calm. This was Blake, the guy I had kissed today. The guy who gave me a heart-shaped stone. Could he really do this and deny he was hurting her? I tried to keep my tone light.

'When did he say that?'

'When it happened.' When *what* happened?

I clutched at the small relief her words brought. She didn't say yesterday, or today, but 'when it happened'. I breathed in deeply and carefully. 'You were too young. You told me you couldn't remember.'

'Once we had an argument'—*once?*—'and I spilt his drink over his good pants. He said I ruin everything. Mum would still be alive if it weren't for me.'

'How old were you?'

'I was in prep. I remember now.' She sounded defensive and I knew she was telling the truth. If she was five, Blake was only fourteen. I could imagine a young, hurting Blake saying angry things he didn't mean. But that was five years ago. Desperately I needed to believe the Blake I knew wasn't like that now.

'I'm sure he doesn't still think that.' I took a breath. 'He must have said it because he was upset. Did he ever say it again?'

She shook her head.

'There you are then.'

But her lower lip came out. 'He said it. He meant it. He must still think it.'

'Then you're going to have to be brave again.'

She stared at me, her lip still protruding. 'Why?'

'Remember how Gul, Begal's sister, felt when she spoke to the king? Maybe you need to say what you feel to Blake.'

'How? What would I say?' She wasn't making it easy, making excuses because she knew it wouldn't work.

'Ask him what he thinks now. Or better still, tell him he had it wrong.'

She sat thinking and I wondered if I'd asked too much. To be able to do all that, she'd have to understand her mother's death wasn't her fault. And what if I was wrong? I didn't know what had happened. I could hear an echo of Blake's voice, *she could do something really weird.* So, she'd drowned the kittens. Was that such a crime? Misguided, but not mean. She didn't enjoy it like a psychopath would.

I sat there, looking at Kerra, who was staring back at me, as I tried not to let my fear show. Even if I was right, and it wasn't her fault, what if she'd believed the lie for too long?

15

The day of the Camel Cup dawned sunny and blue after a cold, cloudless night. I awoke with anticipation. The effect of our road trip the day before hadn't left me. I stretched and felt more relaxed than I had for a long time, with the memory of our kiss and my *let's do it again*. My Pakistani friends would think me *unseemly*. The warmth of our time together made me smile. Even though emotions had flared up easily between Blake and myself during the past week, I expected our relationship to be smoother from now on. Surely Blake would be more understanding towards Kerra too.

I dressed in country clothes for The Cup—jeans, shirt and Mrs Townsend's boots. As I was doing up the laces, I paused, remembering Kerra repeating Blake's words. Was she telling the truth?

I was late getting to the kitchen. Mr Townsend was already cooking porridge.

'Sorry I'm late, Mr Townsend.'

'No worries, love. I usually make it when you're not here.' He smiled at me, but there was an inquiring look in his eyes.

'Hi, Kerra.' She was sitting at the table, watching her dad and her words rose again in my mind. *I ruin everything.*

Mum would still be alive if it weren't for me. She had been only five—surely, she had misunderstood Blake's meaning.

At the race track Blake was full of explanations about the camels, the races and what went on. He smiled at me and his eyes were warm as if he were thinking about our kiss as well.

'Even the army have a camel in the races.'

I watched one lanky camel driver stride down the track, leading his beast to the starting line. His hair was the colour of camel fur and he wore jeans and sweater—a modern camel driver, yet for me he still had that ancient presence of being one with himself and his animal like the first camel drivers.

Blake lifted me up onto a high bench so I could see. 'The camels all have to kneel before the race can start.'

I laughed. As the last camel scrambled down on its haunches—groaning the whole way—a few others promptly stood again. 'They're not very cooperative.'

'Nup. Never know which way they'll run either.'

Like an emu, I thought sombrely.

After the fuss of getting the six camels to kneel, the race was on, before anyone was ready, not even the commentator.

'Oh, here comes Curry on the side. No he's gone west... now it's Priscilla, Queen of the Desert in front...but no, she's worse than a drunken driver...it's Curry again, no, what an idiot, he's stopped to check the oil...' The caller's voice came across the loud speaker, just before the winning camel crossed the finishing line.

'That's it?'

'Yep, it only takes fifteen seconds. Have to be watching

or you miss it.' Blake tipped back my hat. 'They have heats like that all day to see who gets into the Cup Race. C'mon, I'll get you a drink. It'll be ages before they're set up again at the other end.'

'Have you ridden a camel, Blake?'

'Sure. When I was younger I used to race. Too heavy now. Every year we sponsor one of them to race. All the stations help out.'

Just then Zack saw us and brought some of his cousins over to talk. Well, they tried to talk but, even though it wasn't lunch yet, most of them were 'as drunk as skunks', as Blake explained later. 'Great guys,' he said. 'Hearts of gold...do anything for you. They just like their beer.' One of them kept poking me on the shoulder to make sure I was listening, but I couldn't understand his slurred words. If I didn't already know Zack, I would have been uncomfortable, not knowing what to do.

After some time, the guys got interested in the races again and while Blake went to get steak sandwiches for lunch, I wandered back to the benches.

'Jaime.' I swung round to find Zack's mother, grandmother, and heaps of other people, smiling at me. 'These are some of our relatives from Port Agutta,' Zack's mother said. Everyone said hello and by the time they'd all hugged me I couldn't remember their names. Nazzi took my face in her hands and kissed me on the cheek. We're having a party tomorrow night, why don't you come?'

I smiled my thanks and sat beside Nazzi. She was full of her own commentary about the camel races. 'Never seen an ugly brown one like that before. And the handlers take longer and longer getting them down.'

Zack's mother laughed at her. 'Mum, only one thing goes down on time up here, and that's the sun.' Sitting beside Nazzi like that made me want to ask her questions, lots of them. About ageless things, like 'how do you know what you've come from when you're born in a different place?' or 'how do you cope with not knowing?' But she was too happy watching the ridiculous antics of the camels and I didn't want to break her mood.

That afternoon, soon after we'd gone to rented rooms at the pub to change, Kerra came to me dressed in white for the Cup Dance. I was glad. I'd been worried about her since there must have been so much on her mind. Mr Townsend had done his part, in his own quiet way, by the sound of it, but I knew there was a lot more lurking under the surface. She didn't say anything at first, just went over to the dresser and stared out the window.

'She loved me, Mum did.' I stood behind her. It was the first time I'd seen Kerra in a dress. I hoped she wouldn't get cold in the night but I didn't nag her about dressing for the weather, since she seemed happy. She looked like a flaxen princess ready for a ball.

'Yes, and I'm sure she'd want you to be happy.' She looked up at me while she digested that, then I saw the smile. The hug, when it came, was as good as any one of Elly's. It was the first time Kerra had hugged me of her own free will.

'We have lots of time,' she said, prattling almost like Elly would have done, and guiding me to the bed. 'Dad won't be in to get dressed for ages. He's talking to all the other men.' I knew what she was leading up to.

'So you want me to tell you another story?'

She nodded. 'It might be too late tonight. Blake likes to stay out late.'

'Does he?' I guessed if Mr Townsend brought her home, I'd stay at the dance with Blake. The evening stretching ahead was holding all sorts of possibilities. 'Why don't you tell me a story for a change?'

She frowned at me.

'What are you thinking?'

She lifted her shoulders and sighed, too big a sigh for one so young. 'Just that I wished my brother loved me like Prince Hamid loved Princess Noori and like Mr Kimberley loved Liana and Abbas loved…' I let her go on as I realised she'd just called Blake her brother.

'Righto. Everybody ready then?' It was Mr Townsend at the doorway. 'Thought I'd find Kerra in here.' He was shaved and gleaming clean; in his hand was the Akubra that everyone wore up there, even in winter. 'Blake's in the Cruiser.'

That was our cue. Kerra literally jumped off the bed. Mr Townsend watched her, shaking his head. 'First time I've seen her do that in a while.' The look he passed me was one of thanks, as if he thought I'd done it all, worked a miracle. But had I? I suspected her happiness was as fragile as a whisper in the wind.

I wasn't ready for the rush of noise from the band. It was set up on the back of a huge truck on the race course. At first, the figures dancing round the fires looked bizarre against the backdrop of the night sky—like an ancient rite of the

Celts. But when I drew closer, I couldn't wait to join in. Guys in jeans and the hats that never seemed to fall off, girls too, were dancing to country songs round the campfires. The line dancing was wild, the guys with thumbs stuck in the loops of their jeans, concentrating on the steps, the girls laughing, hair swinging. There were tons of people, even tourists from Adelaide and interstate.

Blake led me by the elbow and before I had a chance to sit by a fire, he'd swung me into the dance. It was fun; a lot like the dances Mr Kimberley used to teach us at school in Pakistan, but nothing like the stuff we danced at the Year 12 dinner in Adelaide. It didn't stop, either. Before I knew it we were in another dance, then another that changed partners, like one of those folk dances in primary school, in and out the window, except it was in and around the fires. I was definitely beginning to wilt by the time I reached Matt in the barn dance. He could probably tell by the way I was stepping on his toes and when he said, 'Want to have a rest?' I didn't care if I sounded relieved.

He took me to have a drink in the shed where beer and soft drinks were on sale until ten. I wondered why he didn't take me outside. It would have been cooler.

Instead he indicated chairs, sat down beside me and asked, 'How's it goin'?'

It felt like the night he found me in the scrub. There was so much I wanted to say, knew I could say, but not just then. How easy it would be to have a crush on him; how much simpler life might be with his steady personality. Then I shook myself out of that thought. He was my mate. Blake was the one I liked.

Matt answered his own question. 'Kerra seems happier. I was dancing with her before.'

'You?'

He chuckled. 'Yup. She's quite a kid.'

'She's still a worry, though.'

'Yeah?' It was a question, not his usual grunt. His eyebrows rose.

'You were right, I think, about Blake and Kerra. About it being to do with their mother. But knowing hasn't fixed it. Something still has to be done.'

'But only they can do it, right?'

I took a sip of my juice. 'I think so.'

Blake was there then, pulling me up with a nod at Matt, taking me to supper in the next shed. Halfway through all the egg-and-lettuce sandwiches and party sausage rolls, I wondered how Kerra was doing. No doubt she was with her dad; supper seemed to be on tap and maybe they'd already had theirs. Supper wasn't the only thing I found on tap. Outside, as Blake steered me over to a bench, there were a few whistles and laughs from a group of guys crowded round, drinking from green tins.

Blake laughed. 'Sure. Some of them will get drunk, but most of them are just having fun.'

'Have you seen Kerra?' I supposed I shouldn't have started our time alone with Kerra but I was worried by then. I had a fleeting thought that maybe our peaceful day out was due to me not mentioning Kerra. He hadn't seen her, nor did he seem very concerned about it.

'You worry too much about her,' was all he said, like she'd been okay before I came. I almost bristled, then calmed myself and asked him a question instead. I was still riding on the closeness I felt with him from the day before.

'Blake, when your mum died, did you think it was Kerra's fault?'

He sighed, as though lifting a heavy stone, and stretched out his legs. I had a sudden vision of the fight we had at the gorge, but I couldn't leave it alone, not after the stuff Kerra had been saying.

When Blake did speak I almost jumped.

'Yeah, I did. But I was barely thirteen years old. Sure, I thought it was her fault, but not only hers. If I'd been there, it would have been different. Maybe if I'd been home, if it were holidays—'

'If you'd never gone away to school?'

'That too, I guess. But I knew I had to go to school. It's just stuff you think about. What if, what if.'

'Kerra feels guilty about it too, like it was all her fault.'

'What can I do?' I heard his defensiveness rise like a castle drawbridge. 'I can't turn back the clock.'

I didn't care that he'd raised the bridge, I jumped into the cold water anyway. 'You could give her a second chance. Don't you think five years is long enough to bear a grudge? Kerra is just a kid.'

He looked at me as if I'd said arsenic wouldn't kill because it came in a lolly jar. It shocked me, to find that the blame was still present. But I could see Kerra, scared and defenceless, and I knew it was tied up with him.

'Maybe you don't outright blame her now, but what if that thirteen-year-old boy in there still does. No kid deserves to believe she's evil like Kerra—'

He stood up, the movement sudden, tipping the bench back. 'Yesterday I thought you were beginning to understand—' He stopped. 'Look, what's done is done. Just leave it alone!'

I thought he'd be annoyed, but nothing prepared me for the look on his face. It was more than anger, there was hurt and pain as well.

'I don't have to justify myself to you, but you're so wrong. I don't consciously think it's her fault. That'd be dumb…it's if she gets in my face…it's just a feeling I get. It's the way things are.'

I didn't try to be gentle. 'Surely it's not the way things have to be.' Maybe it was grief that had never been worked out. But there was Kerra, so young, she didn't know how to cope with all the feelings she had.

Blake was too quiet, his arms crossed, eyes shut. His whole body was taut and I knew deep inside he wasn't quiet at all. His meaning was clear: subject closed. It unnerved me.

If I'd said all that to my friend, Jasper, I think he would have ranted and raved even more, maybe got over it quickly, but I sure would have heard about it. But this was worse than the picnic at the gorge; this was a Blake who was so upset he didn't even trust himself to speak to me, maybe never would again. I'd lost something I wanted, but how could I have a relationship with him when there was so much that couldn't be talked about? The place he wouldn't let me in would affect everything we did together. Would even yesterday have ended like this if I'd mentioned Kerra?

I didn't even touch him as I went back to the bonfires. I headed towards the music and dancing but I didn't make it to the race track. There was this apparition, dancing all by itself, outside in the shadows, humming. Kerra. I watched her for a while. She hadn't worn a jumper and the white dress made her look like a flower piskey. Her aloneness tugged at my soul, paralysed me so I couldn't break into her spell.

She saw me as she twirled and stopped, breathless and smiling. The smile made her a child again and I found my voice.

'What are you doing over here?'

She didn't seem a child as she answered. 'Need you ask? I'm practising my dancing to save Blake. Like Liana saved her brother and you.'

Her tone and the way she had remembered such a detail, when I'd said so little about it, made me nervous. I tried to laugh but it came out as a croak. 'Those are just stories—' I didn't get any further, as she danced closer.

'Or I can be like Mariama. I could save Blake like she saved Abbas in the storm.'

What did Kerra think she was going to do now? Just save Blake? How would she do that? I wondered then if it was ever possible to save anyone without dying in some way first.

I took her by the hand. 'Don't you think we should dance by the fires where it's warm?' I felt like going home. Nothing had turned out like I'd expected. My first country dance: I'd had visions of dancing with Blake at midnight, coming home at some unearthly hour, kisses in the garden, maybe even fall in love. Now I knew it was finished.

When we found Mr Townsend to go home, the last thing I saw was Richelle leading Blake into the dancing; the music was quieter and I was determined not to cry. Let her cheer him up after I'd pulled him down—she was his mate, wasn't she? What did I care? But as I rode home in the back of the Cruiser I realised I did care. Too much.

16

Blake wasn't around the next morning. I was glad. There was nothing more to say. Kerra had already gone by the time I woke. It had been so late when we arrived home that she and I had dropped off in my bed. If Mr Townsend noticed how quiet I was when he came in mid-morning, he didn't comment on it, only asked if I'd enjoyed the dance.

'It was different from what I expected,' was all I said. That was true, at least. He went out after his smoko, back to finish stacking the hundred bales of hay he'd ordered in for horse feed.

'We need rain,' was his parting comment.

The morning got more depressing as it wore on. Richelle turned up. I had expected a run-in with her. Even though the last time she came she seemed more accepting of me, I knew she must still be wary of me. You can sense things like that about people just the way you can tell if you're being stared at. Also, she was a thermometer when it came to Blake's wellbeing.

I made all the right sounds and motions; got out the coffee, salty crackers with cheese, pickled onions and pepper, the way the Townsends liked them. She looked civil but I sensed there was a lot on her mind. She couldn't keep her hands still. The trivia about the camel races didn't last long.

'And you, Jaime, what do you think you're up to?' She suddenly came out with it as if she'd caught me stealing from the station safe.

'What do you mean?' She breathed heavily, only just managing to stay calm.

'Blake was fine all the other times he came home, before you arrived. Now he's flipping all over the place.'

'That's not my fault. There's stuff he needs to—'

'Bullshit!' Her calm shattered. 'You're an interfering bitch. This is *our* life. Who do you think you are to come and dig up stuff like this? To ruin everything.' She was nothing like Matt. He didn't share her view, did he? He said Blake should talk; that it may as well be to me.

'But—'

'He was doing fine. He'd put it all away. It has to be forgotten, you have to get on with life. Then you come along, you'—she even clenched her fists—'you know nothing. You weren't even here. Just because you thought you liked the look of him at school.'

That stung. She made me sound like a thirteen-year-old airhead. I wanted the best for Blake, though I wasn't about to tell her that, and the knowledge spurred me into defence.

'You can't sweep stuff under the carpet. Look at the way Blake treats Kerra—'

'She's a brat. He's a good brother. No one's ever understood what he's been through. And Kerra was just a little kid. She wouldn't even remember what happened.'

Richelle had to be wrong. No one had ever bothered to find out what Kerra thought of it all.

'I think she does.' I believed what I said, knew that even if Kerra didn't understand all that happened, she remembered how people felt at the time. But it sounded improbable and Richelle stared at me as if I were muttering insanities.

'And all that stupid storytelling.' How'd she know about that? 'You're just dumping all your shit onto Blake and Kerra.'

I was determined not to get sidetracked. 'Kerra doesn't even know who she is; she's depressed, believed a lie for so long. Blake too. They need to talk about it, let it go, not hide it.'

'What utter crap! Everybody knows who they are, they just need to get on with life. You've stirred Kerra up for nothing, that's all you've done.'

I knew she was sticking up for Blake the way a mate would, like I should've too. No wonder she didn't think I cared for him. I did, but that didn't mean I had to pretend he was perfect, did it? Couldn't I still like him, yet not accept every single thing he did? And aren't friends meant to sharpen each other up?

'You've caused so much trouble. And I bet there's more coming. You can't stir up a nest of bush bees without being stung.'

Richelle flounced off soon after that. Her depth of feeling shocked me, the message clear: lay off Blake. The tears came, and I was glad I hadn't cried in front of her. The encounter made me think for a long time, not because I thought she was right, but because I realised I felt more for Blake than I'd thought. It wasn't just wanting the best for him, I wanted something for me too. And Kerra. I couldn't explain it but I felt the fear for Kerra woven in with what I felt for Blake, wondering if his love would ever be shown in the way I wanted. His ability to let me close seemed frustrated by his response to Kerra, as though there was a gate he had to break down before he was free to care for me.

Was Richelle right? Did my grief for Liana really cause me to get onto Blake too much? Was I the one who was so insecure that I pushed him away, always bringing up Kerra so we'd fight? Maybe I was afraid of losing someone again. Yet Liana was always with me; when I was upset, she still figured in my thoughts. Though as time went on, the thought of her was less shadowy, less depressing. It wasn't her death that wrung me out anymore, just the knowledge of what I'd lost. Now the good times I had with Liana came to mind more readily.

I didn't see Blake at all that day. For all I knew he'd ridden off with Richelle, but at tea time Mr Townsend told me Blake had gone shooting dingoes by the Fence; he'd be back late. I heard what he was saying: no use waiting up for him. I wouldn't anyway. I needed space to think, and I couldn't with Blake there. Whatever his mood, he could influence me.

After tea I went to my room to check emails and messages. I was tired of being with my thoughts all day of what I should (or shouldn't) have said to Blake; wondering if he hated me now. There was a message from Elly she'd written on Mum's iPhone.

I have so many mice now, Jammie. The white mum just had another batch of babies. Dad calls them batches. I'll need a new glass box for them soon, but Dad says I should sell some to the pet shop in Parabanks and start a business.

I could hear the squeals and giggles between her words. Dear uncomplicated Elly who everyone loved.

Soon after, Kerra climbed onto my bed. She brought her drawing book.

'I miss Sasha,' she said.

I put an arm around her. 'It's hard when we lose a friend.' I thought of Elly; she'd be devastated if she lost her mice. 'What about a mouse for a pet?'

She looked at me as if to say, 'Duh'. 'Dad says they're pests.'

'Of course.' I blew out a breath.

'Do you want to see my drawings?'

'Sure.' I noticed the one she had been drawing on the windmill platform. She'd finished the colour. 'These are good, Kerra.' She turned the page. This one looked like a horse again; it was hard to tell as the whole page was black. I drew in a quiet breath, trying to calm myself. *It's just a picture, Jaime,* but still I asked, 'Why is it all black?'

Kerra pursed her lips. 'Because it's night time, silly.' I didn't feel as relieved as I should have.

I leaned back against the pillows. 'I have another story.' She brightened. 'You might have heard it before.'

'That doesn't matter,' she said more kindly.

I told her the story of Joseph, how his brothers hated him because he was favoured and had a multi-coloured robe. They tried to kill him but instead, sold him to camel traders who took him to Egypt. He was falsely accused of a crime, put in prison, had dreams. He could interpret other people's dreams too and this talent finally got him released since he told the pharaoh what his disturbing dream was about.'

'A drought was coming,' Kerra supplied. 'One so bad that all the countries in the area would have no crops, no food, no cattle. Even the dead finish bushes would die in that.'

'Yes. But Joseph was clever and he had a plan. He advised the pharaoh to collect grain for seven years in readiness for the drought.' Kerra nodded. 'The pharaoh made him governor of all Egypt, so his plan could be carried out. Then the drought hit.'

'And his brothers came for grain.'

'You know it?'

'Mum told me.'

I held my breath. Was Kerra truly beginning to remember?

'She told me a story from the Bible every night. Sometimes she read it but she could tell it the way you do. Mum was like you.'

I frowned. Is that why Kerra was drawn to me; why Blake was attracted to me? I was like their mum?

'Do you remember what happened between Joseph and his brothers?' I asked.

She fiddled with her book. 'They were frightened of him because they thought he'd hate them.'

'Did he punish them?'

She shook her head. 'He let them off the hook, forgave them.' She looked up at me with such yearning in her eyes.

'It can be hard to forgive someone,' I said, slowly, 'but after time we feel better if we do. It's like untangling ourselves from a knot.'

It was a while before Kerra spoke again and I let her be;

I was finally used to people round there speaking only when they felt like it. It had seemed bad manners at first, but now I accepted it as a habit from another culture.

'I'll do something one day, so Blake loves me, you'll see.' Her words left me cold and not for the first time I regretted the way I'd changed some of the stories for Kerra. I'd only done it so she could see a brother could be special, a brother could love and be loved. I hadn't counted on her wanting Blake's response rather than working on her own feelings.

The generator had long stopped its beating and Blake wasn't home yet. I tucked Kerra under the quilt and read by the light of the oil lamp.

17

In the morning I realised Blake must have come back in the night. Even though I swore to myself I wasn't doing it, I lay awake, listening for the ute, praying he'd be okay in more ways than one. When I entered the kitchen he was there, making coffee. He even said, 'Hi'. How could he do that? Didn't he feel the rift between us? I could sense a chasm yawning at my feet.

'How was the shooting?' was all I said when really I wanted to know how he was. Did he still like me? What did he think about Kerra now?

'Fine. Got three.'

'Hang them on the Fence?'

'Yeah. Jaime—' He looked up then, stepped closer. I wasn't sure I could stand it: what if he didn't mean that expression on his face. 'I've been thinking.' He put his arms around me while I steeled myself not to ask anything, not to spoil the moment. His kiss when it came was soft, gentle, no hint of the anger and passion of the other night at the Cup Dance. It made me feel peculiar, as if he wanted comfort, was saying sorry, and cared for me too.

He never got to tell me what he'd been thinking, as his father came in for a coffee.

Mr Townsend didn't seem to notice how close we'd been standing, just said, 'It's chilly outside.' He was a master at understatement; actually, the wind was freezing.

Blake seemed relaxed like he had on our day out, said he'd take me to Zack's place for the BBQ I'd been invited to at the races. In the ute I was careful not to say anything I shouldn't, not because of what Richelle had said but, because I didn't want to lose the renewed communication we seemed to have. Whether talking is truly communing when you're ignoring what's on your mind, I chose not to examine.

It seemed all of Zack's family were at his grandmother's house and I was shy of intruding at first. But the one thing they did have in common with Afghans in Afghanistan was their easy hospitality. Soon Blake was laughing with one of Zack's friends, green can in hand and I was eating sausages and sauce next to Nazzi, the oldest lady there.

This time I asked her the question that had burned in me last time I saw her. I was watching Zack telling some joke to the guys. We could hear the swearing and laughing even from where I was sitting by Nazzi.

'Zack is Afghan, so how come he—?' I couldn't put it into words. I wanted to know how they kept who they were. They were Afghan descendants but Zack was nothing like the Afghans I knew. Did that mean he wasn't one because he didn't act like one? Nazzi was pretty astute, maybe she'd seen the confusion in my face, because she seemed to follow the tangle of my thoughts.

'Zack doesn't have a sense of being Afghan, love. He only

knows it in his head. He's Nunga, one of the Marree mob now. Even that's hard, most of the local people have lost who they were too.'

'How do you keep who you are?'

'I can't tell you, love. It can take eighty years sometimes. For me, it's what I believe inside that keeps me who I am. We are all visitors to this time, this place. We are just passing through. Our purpose here is to observe, to learn, to grow, to love…and then we return home.'

'Doesn't it matter who we are?'

She smiled. 'You have to tell yourself the truth because if you don't, you become a shadow, changing shape every time the sun shifts.'

I wanted to ask more about Zack, but she kept going as if she thought I was asking for myself. 'Be patient. I'm sure the caterpillar wonders what it will be before it flies and once it does, I bet it's never bothered by the problem again.'

One of the relatives came up to sit with Nazzi. I moved over, feeling in the way. Maybe they all only got to see her once a year and here I was, a stranger, taking up her time. Blake was into his second piece of steak before he noticed I'd gone quiet. He took me home soon after that. I appreciated his concern; it was always there for me, I knew that. It was just so confusing how he could change when Kerra was around. Was he like Zack too? Zack gave me the impression he didn't know where he fitted. Kerra also gave me that impression, although I was sure she'd be more settled if she and Blake could sort out their feelings.

Kerra was nowhere in the house when we returned in the afternoon and I was just wondering which cubby hole she'd be in—the chook shed, the stables, hayloft, the windmill, the tree in the garden—when I smelled smoke. I wasn't the only one for I could hear shouting and Mr Townsend driving the ute down to the home paddock. Blake raced into the kitchen.

'Ring Matt. Quick!'

'What's wrong?'

But Blake was out the door already. 'Tell him the haystack's burning,' he shouted as he sped off.

Mulga Spring was on a party line with Bulcanna; two short rings and one long one. What if Matt wasn't there? Wouldn't he be working?

Mrs Hall answered. 'Goodness, how awful, love. I'll send Richelle for Matt right away.'

I managed to staunch Mrs Hall's discussion on how a haystack could possibly burn in winter; she seemed to make up for all the talking the men didn't do round there. I hung up as politely as I could and raced out to see what I could do to help.

Mr Townsend already had the ute with forty-four-gallon drums on the tray, siphoning water out of a hose onto the burning hay. Blake was banging at the ground around the stack with a wet hessian bag.

'Get a bag!' He motioned to the ute. I followed his example and wet the bag in one of the drums and tried beating at the flames like he was. This wasn't a bushfire but the heat coming off the stack and the smoke hanging round us still made it difficult to breathe. There wasn't time to think. Blake beat a path all the way round the stack, to stop the fire spreading. I went the other way, beating, pushing hair out of my face, and when we met, we didn't even speak, just went back the other way, dipping the bags in a drum when we could. Blake looked like a chimney sweep with soot and grime dribbling down his face in the sweat. I wouldn't have looked much better.

When Matt and Richelle arrived with their fire-fighting trailer, complete with tank and wide hoses, we had already made a fire break. With both vehicles it wasn't long before the fire was out. It seemed small consolation to me as I surveyed the damage with Blake and Matt. Their faces were grim and even though I understood little about life up there, I knew how important a haystack was in that climate. No hay, no feed for the horses or the stock.

'How'd you think it started?' Matt was standing with Blake. There was discussion about the sun, glass, matches, someone throwing a cigarette from a car window—but we were so far off the beaten track—how hay goes up like tinder in a match box. I wondered why they bothered until I heard the word 'insurance'. Of course, they'd need to recoup the damage and be able to prove it was an accident. It wasn't until later that Mr Townsend explained how hay will suddenly combust if it wasn't dry enough when it was brought in. But by then it was too late.

Blake bent down. 'What's this?' No one spoke as he held up one of Kerra's hair clasps, blackened, but I recognised it. So did he; I heard him mutter her name. I hoped he didn't think she had anything to do with the fire just because he'd found a clip. She could have dropped it anytime. But just then, before I could say so, Kerra had the misfortune of showing up.

She seemed different, defensive but confident, as if she was ready to take on the world.

'Where have *you* been?' Was Blake's creative opening.

I took a step forward but Matt held me back and I heard his low murmur, 'It's between them.'

'You've been playing down here, haven't you?'

'Sometimes.'

'Today?'

'No.'

'So you're telling stories now.'

Kerra's face had that blank stubborn set to it. *Think what you want, if that's all you care.*

'You've been playing with matches.' It wasn't even a question, and suddenly Kerra lashed out.

'You're wrong! You're always wrong. I didn't do it. I never do half the stuff you think I do. Even the stuff you tell me off for is wrong.' Blake walked towards her then. Matt still had hold of my arm and I watched the look on Blake's face with mounting apprehension. It wasn't much different from the look I'd seen on a stockman's face riding a bucking colt at the muster. He'd ridden it out until he'd won.

'You can't bully me anymore, either! And I didn't kill Mum.'

Blake stopped close to her. She didn't move.

'What the hell—? Where did that come from?' He frowned across at me and I knew he thought I'd put her up to saying it. I shook off Matt's hand. But just as I was about to stride over to them, Mr Townsend strolled up. We didn't know how much he'd heard but he basically told Blake to shove off. Then he ordered Kerra to get up to the house where he'd sort it all out. I followed her.

They didn't get to sort it out then. Kerra seemed calm enough. I didn't for a minute think she'd lit the fire but that feeling of being misunderstood is very painful and could make someone—even if they weren't like Kerra—act out of character. I should've watched her better.

She was in my room and looked up as I came in from the bathroom. She must have been doing some serious thinking for she plunged straight in with a deep and meaningful question. 'Why doesn't Blake love me?'

'I'm sure he does.' But how kids see through platitudes.

'No, he doesn't. Or he'd know I didn't set the fire.'

'He was upset from losing all the feed.'

'He didn't need to take it out on me. He always does. I wish he could forget how bad he thinks I am.' And then I understood that in loving him she only wanted his love in return.

'Why don't you tell him that? That's what you need to say'—and I added, hoping I wasn't wrong—'tell him you love him. Maybe he doesn't know. You'll be surprised what a difference it'll make, like setting something free.' I trusted I wasn't getting her hopes up for nothing, but Blake was a good guy. Surely, he wouldn't be able to resist a child's faith.

'Like the kitten, Jaime?'

'Yes. You gave him a second chance. Do the same for Blake.'

'Like Joseph too.'

My eyes were blurry by then. Kerra wiped my cheek with her finger. 'Why are you crying?'

'Because you're a special girl.' I don't think she'd been told that very often because her smile was condescending, like, *how would you know?*

She just said, 'I'd rather write a note. When I try to talk to Blake it comes out wrong.'

I gave her some paper from my backpack.

Kerra didn't say anymore, just turned to the paper and began printing, her tongue protruding slightly. I patted her on the shoulder and went down to the kitchen; whatever was happening, everyone still had to be fed.

The vegetables were steaming on top of the stove by the time Blake came through the kitchen. He'd washed most of the soot and grime off in the laundry, but he was still a sight. I gave him a tentative smile and watched him. He didn't walk straight through and I guessed he wanted to talk, but I'd learnt not to push him. Even though he didn't look angry, I could see his chest straining like floodwater against a weakened dam. I waited.

Finally he got it out. 'I'm going roo shooting. Taking Bow.' I was thinking of the letter Kerra was writing, how it might help.

'Why don't you wait a while—' But he was too distracted to listen.

He didn't say much else, just, 'I've got to get away. To think. It was never this bad.'

Richelle's words returned to taunt me. Did he think I'd stirred up trouble too? And even though I believed it was good that Kerra was starting to think for herself and to stand up to him, I said sorry, and reached out an arm towards him.

To my surprise he responded, actually put his arms round me. I hung on, knowing it wasn't the type of holding the girls at school always talked about, but an earthy stand-by-your-mate-whatever-the-cost kind of hug. Kerra wasn't the only one with a dragon in the closet to clear out. Blake had one too.

18

Blake strode out to the ute to pack for his shooting trip that night. I watched him through the kitchen window, saw him take the gun from inside the cabin, check it, and put it on the tray while he yanked out a small box from behind the driver's seat. I didn't dare go near him; he was in another world, shoving gear in the ute, throwing other stuff out. Guess he just needed time to cool off.

After that moment it all happened so fast. Kerra came round from the back of the house. She couldn't have known he was there because she stopped dead just a few feet from him.

'Blake—' I heard her plea, almost a whimper, cracked and hesitant. It was the first I'd ever heard her reach out to him like that. I held my breath, in dread, hoping for her sake he'd hear her and understand. Yet, I knew what she couldn't at her age, that it wasn't the right time, not with him throwing empty shells out of the box as if hoping they'd ignite and erase all the trouble.

'Blake.'

He turned then. 'What do you want now?'

Even I flinched. I couldn't imagine what his tone did to

Kerra but she kept on. Maybe what she wrote in the note was fresh in her mind.

'I want you to be my brother.'

'What?' For a moment his mouth dropped and he looked odd, as if he was trying to understand, but it passed as he shook his head. 'You've got a weird way of looking at things.' He turned back to the open door of the ute, shutting her out. But Kerra hadn't finished. Guess that was when everything snapped in her head, and when I came face to face with the horror of what my storytelling had led to.

All the trying through the years to get him to notice her, to care, and nothing worked. And now she'd asked, wanted to let him in, but he wouldn't come. She stepped forward, too fast for me to realise what was in her mind, too fast to get out there in time, to warn him. I saw her pick up the rifle off the tray, lift it, stagger slightly under the weight, level it at Blake. In the same instant I was out the kitchen door but I couldn't shout, not like at the dam when she drowned the kittens.

Blake had turned. He'd seen her now. He was speaking. 'Give me the gun.'

His tone was still that of a big brother, as if he knew she'd hand it over as soon as he asked. Did he really believe she'd do what he said with the gun in her hands? When would he see that all she wanted was *him*, his arms around her, his love, his forgiveness.

'I'm going to save us. You're not fair. I didn't do it, not the haystack, not anything. Not Mum. Honey fell. It was cold. She wouldn't get off Mum. I tried and tried to pull her off. Mum was screaming and I hurt too. But I didn't do it. It was an accident!'

'Kerra! It's all right.' I heard my own words delayed and echoing like a person gassed.

'Kerra! Noo!' Was that Blake yelling or me? It didn't stop her; she couldn't hear. She squeezed the trigger. That click was the loudest and slowest sound I'd ever heard. It reverberated in my head more deafening than any gunfire I'd heard in Afghanistan. For a second Blake didn't react. Then he slumped against the side of the ute.

Kerra dropped the gun, tears streaming down her cheeks, the look on her face saying, *Now I really am bad. What are you going to do about that!* Before she ran off, she turned back to him. 'Why can't you just love me? Do things with me, like everyone else's brother?'

Then came the sobs. When a guy cries like that he probably wants to be alone, but I couldn't leave. I knew it wasn't from fear, or that he could've died as Kerra had no way of knowing the gun was unloaded. He saw me standing in front of him. Should I find his father, or call Matt? I did neither. I went to Blake. His arms closed round me as I heard the whispered words, 'What have I done?' And I heard the unspoken question between each of them: *How could she hate me that much?*

It wasn't hate. Hate, love—they could be close, but I didn't speak. It was too big. All I could do was hold him. I loved him, I knew that now, but I was holding a shell. I prayed he'd come together again, to be the real Blake I thought I knew.

It was later, when he came to my room that we knew Kerra had gone. He sat there on my bed, Kerra's note in one hand.

'And why Cador?' I almost heard his 'Kerra' tone again.

'She's done it again. Always goading me, doing things she knows I don't like.'

I took a breath. 'She only does things to get you to notice, to see if you'll care.' Even though I believed that, I also wondered if she took Blake's horse for insurance, to make sure he'd come. But he had to decide that himself. I knew he could be hard, maybe being brought up on the land made people tough, but what if he couldn't see that he had to go after her? What if he thought there was no danger, that she'd come back when she was ready? She wouldn't come back. If she could walk into a dam to get him to love her, kill those kittens that 'deserved to die'...What if she decided she did too? If Blake didn't go, we might never find the happy Kerra that must be buried inside her.

Shame and guilt were as plain on his face as the letter chart on a doctor's wall and I wished I could rip it off.

'Never got to say goodbye,' was all he said at first and I knew he wasn't talking about Kerra. 'Never got to say anything, say how much I'd missed her. But this time I'll be there. I'll go after her.' At first I stiffened; he'd switched to Kerra. Was this the bossy big brother again, taking vent on his little sister? Then I relaxed as he spoke again. 'We never knew that about Honey. Kerra never said. She never said anything afterwards, like if she did it would make the horror real, I guess. I felt the same. Even though I wasn't there. Dad told me all he knew.'

'What happened?' I asked gently.

'Kerra was four. I had just started high school in Adelaide. I lived with my aunt. Kerra was always a handful. Dad called it free spirited, like with horses. He used to say she needed a bit of rein. Even then she liked to roam, except it's dangerous when you're little.

'One time it'd rained'—Blake made that sound like it only happened once in five years—'and we'd found her footprints in the mud. She was two then, been dragging her wagon along the road through the water and when all the deep puddles came, she'd swerved and missed them. She couldn't have known the water was deeper there. It was God looking after her, I guess, but it freaked Mum out. Kerra could've drowned. Mum watched her closely after that, kept her in the garden to play.

'One day, Kerra learned how to open the gate. When Mum couldn't find her, she was beside herself. Dad was bringing the cattle in and didn't know, wasn't near the two-way. So Mum saddled up Honey and set out herself. Mum was a good horsewoman...there was no reason for it to happen like it did. It was just the freak weather.'

'What sort of weather?'

He swallowed. 'Two-year drought, then that terrible hailstorm. Strange. We lost most our lambs in that. Lot of sheep too.' He stopped and I knew it wasn't all that they lost, and I blinked my eyes to keep them dry. He didn't need my tears.

'They weren't far from the Fence. We still don't know how Kerra got that far. When Dad found them, Mum had Kerra, she'd shielded her, was keeping her warm. The hailstones were too big. We thought maybe she'd fallen. Maybe the stones hit her. Honey was down too. Almost frozen. We didn't know Honey had rolled on her. No wonder...' The words came as phrases, disjointed, like they hurt on the way out. 'No help either. The flying doctor…by the time Dad got them back to the house…everybody else had problems…weren't enough pilots or planes. Twenty-four hours before they finally arrived.' His words were ragged and sharp, and I felt as if I was looking in where no one had before.

'It was too late. The exposure,' he added with a force that belied his quiet voice and I felt his pain as I saw an image of his mother dying, a tiny Kerra trying to help.

'What about you?' I whispered.

'Too late. I flew home from Adelaide for the funeral. Mum and I were like one soul looking out of the same eyes. Dad said it was a wrench for her to send me away in the first place. He said there was nothing I could have done, he was here and still it happened. But maybe I would've gone after Kerra. It might have been different.' I touched his arm.

'She was a special woman, Mum. Strong, saw God's goodness in everybody. Nothing got her down for long.' I looked up at him quickly, and I couldn't help thinking he needed to say all this to Kerra. He was quiet then, far away, until I heard the sobs again. 'And all this time…we never knew…Kerra pulled Honey off Mum. She must have kept Mum alive long enough till Dad got there. All this time I thought if only she hadn't run off—' He stopped then, wiped his eyes.

'I know it wasn't her fault. It just felt like it sometimes, but I never knew I was still doing it.'

'Blaming her?'

He stood up. 'Hell, I'm a jerk.' Then he paused, thinking. 'Maybe if I tell her, it could change, for both of us.'

He hugged me then, kissed me too, and he groaned as

his mouth slipped from mine onto my cheek. 'Jaime, I have to find her. If I don't—' I knew what he meant, that it would be so much worse if anything happened to her as well, but I understood, too, what Kerra would be thinking. She'd be remembering the stories of the brothers looking for their sisters, she would be waiting for him to come, and instantly I took off the silver ring I wore, the half of the puzzle ring I'd given to Kerra.

'Blake, take this. This will sound weird but give it to her.' Blake wasn't too wrapped with the ring, but he put it in his pocket. He was only an image of the Blake I knew, all the vitality and energy gone, looking at me yet not seeing me. It felt like a test of how strong real love is: could I still love him with all his stuffing knocked out of him?

I reached up, stroked the hair back from his forehead. 'Don't worry, you'll find her.' I hoped I sounded convincing.

After Blake went, it didn't take me long to unearth Mr Townsend; he was down at the horse yards. I was breathless when I reached him. He looked up from brushing the Arab, his face asking me the question that anyone else would've asked aloud and I replied, 'Kerra's gone!'

'How do you reckon that?'

'She and Blake had an argument.' I didn't feel like explaining it all. 'You haven't seen her? Since the haystack?'

'Nup. I thought you were keeping her low, like out of my way. Wasn't necessary, I wouldn't have belted her.'

He turned to saddle his horse. 'You better saddle up Rainmaker.' I started off towards Rainmaker's stall. 'Uh, Jaime? Meet you at the house.'

When I finally got Rainmaker saddled (no mean feat

without Blake to coach me) and arrived back at the house, Mr Townsend had already rung Bulcanna. 'Pity Blake's away,' he muttered as he flowed into the saddle and flicked the reins over the Arab's neck.

'Blake's gone to find her on the bike. He thinks she'll be out near the Dog Fence.'

'That so? Then we'll check the west.'

The sun was hanging low, fat and growing pink. There were only the two of us and I was scared. What if I wasn't good enough at riding? What if we didn't find her in time? A thousand square kilometres is a big area to comb and night was coming on—wouldn't there be exposure? Maybe a rogue dingo? What if we never found her? It was as though Mr Townsend could read my thoughts and he pulled his Arab close to Rainmaker.

'Matt'll bring Zack, lass. He can track an ant on cement.'

My mouth twisted into a grin. With Mr Townsend, if it wasn't understatement, it was hyperbole. But my grin soon faded; Mr Townsend was as scared as I was, I could tell by his crooked smile.

We went to the dam first. I don't know how Mr Townsend could do it, but he put his stallion through most of it, checking. When he was satisfied he decided we should split. I was to go down to the gorge where Blake took me for that disastrous first picnic and ride up and down the creek.

'You won't get lost, lass, if you stay within cooee of the creek.' Then he gave me a .22 rifle. 'If you find her, or need anything, give two shots.' And he showed me how to squeeze the trigger, and to keep the safety catch on until I was ready to do it. It took a full minute while the Arab pranced on the spot. Mr Townsend held my gaze. I didn't want to split up, but without Blake, what could we do? So I swallowed the fear and smiled. He seemed satisfied, tipped his hat and was off in a cloud of dust and clatter of little stones.

Rainmaker and I headed to the creek. I called for Kerra until my voice was a croak, trying not to think about whether she took water or food. The creek didn't look a lot different from the day I was there with Blake, except I found a spot further on with water. It was low and alive with algae but Rainmaker stopped to drink. Listening to the calming sounds of her bridle clinking against her cheek made me wish I could forget the thought of what we mightn't find.

19

Kerra wasn't at the gorge. Mr Townsend didn't find her either. He came across me again just as it was getting too dark to see and we headed back to the house. Matt and Richelle were there and plans were laid for a full search at dawn. I raised my eyebrows ready to question this when Mr Townsend said, 'No point you all getting lost in the dark. That won't help Kerra.' I bet he'd go out by himself though. Finally Mr Townsend radioed the Flying Doctor to be on standby and also a neighbouring station that had a small plane. I was to keep within cooee of the radio while everyone else went out to search in the morning.

That night I couldn't sit with the others. Zack kept turning his hat round and round in his hands. I caught Matt's understanding glance on me when I stood to go to bed early. Richelle was cool, her gaze reminding me we'd have more trouble, everything being my fault, of course. I lay in bed, trying to imagine where Kerra would be and would she be scared? Would she be eating those snotty gobbles that she'd told me about when she took me to the dam that first time? Would Blake find her, and if he did, what if they still couldn't get it right and they had another bust up?

I texted my family to pray. I didn't remember sleeping but woke early before the sun had started its decorating. It was the same time I used to wake up for weeks after Liana was killed, early, and I'd find myself sobbing uncontrollably. In time, my sobbing changed to what Pakistanis call weeping and that's what I did this morning: wept and prayed for Kerra and Blake and all that had happened to them and all they'd need to do to have a normal relationship again.

The waiting was hell. The others went at first light. The mailman came in his van. I had no news for him. Nor he for me. I didn't even collect the eggs. What if the radio called while I was in the yard? The time when Mr Townsend would have come in for lunch came and passed. He called once on the two-way. He'd taken the ute; said he'd tried most of the water run within the range he thought Kerra could be and was going to see if Blake needed help near the Fence. I sat there after he'd said, 'over', just staring into space, my mind a husk.

The phone rang. I raced over to it. Maybe someone had found her. It was Mrs Hall. 'Any news, love?'

'No.' She was kind as she went on but I couldn't concentrate. All I could think was someone might be trying to ring to tell me Kerra had been found. I kept listening for the two-way. When Mrs Hall got tired of talking to herself and hung the phone up, I tried doing mundane jobs, peeling spuds for a potato salad. There was cold lamb left in the fridge (as always). I took two loaves of bread out of the freezer, opened a big tin of beetroot. Lots of people would need to be fed. I prayed aloud while buttering bread. 'Please let Kerra be found. Please, God, let her be alive.'

When I heard the roar of the bike and Bow's sharp excited bark, I raced out the kitchen door. Did he find her? I was too scared to look at first, and then I saw them: Kerra perched in front of Blake, Bow on the back, balancing himself ready to jump. There was an aura about them that stopped my wild flight outside to welcome them home. They were quiet but there was a peace, an easiness that I'd never sensed when they'd been together before.

As they came in, I stood at the door, smiling, feeling awkward. There was so much I wanted to say, how happy I was, but I couldn't find the words. They hardly seemed to notice me even though Blake gave me a hug and Kerra smiled at me. She had the full ring on her finger, the silver hand clasp that said it all. Kerra was ravenous and I let them get on with lunch. Mr Townsend rushed in and picked up Kerra. He held her for ages, his shoulders shaking.

I reached Matt on the two-way. Then I rang Mrs Hall.

'I'm so sorry I was distracted before,' I began.

'She's found.' It wasn't even a question.

'Yes, well and happy.' Tears welled up. 'And hungry.' My voice squeaked on 'hungry'.

I heard Mrs Hall's sob. 'Praise the Lord,' she whispered.

It was Kerra who said to me as she crawled into my bed that night, 'He does love me.' She whispered it as though the knowledge was so new it might disappear like a shadow when the sun's high. 'He was looking for me. I saw him, and when he found me, he cried.' The wonder in her voice tore me up, not only to share her joy but also from sadness that it had to be this way. 'He doesn't think I'm bad, either. I wasn't, you know.'

'No.'

'And now I'm going to have a sister too.'

'Who?'

'You, silly. Blake loves you too. You know what that means.'

I laughed at the innocence she revealed at times. If only everything were that simple. And I wondered how she knew anyway; had Blake told her? I hugged her tight and she didn't seem to mind.

'We'll see what happens. Things like that take a lot of time.' And a lot of effort, I reminded myself.

She pulled away then. 'I didn't do anything special though, like Mariama or Gul. I have the ring, my brother, everything that Liana got, but he saved me. He was the one. I didn't save him. I tried to shoot him.' I heard the echo of the way she used to talk and I pulled her close again. She didn't need another problem to beat herself up about.

'If you're sorry about that, it's finished with. Don't worry anymore.' Then I chuckled. 'You did save Blake in a way.'

'How?'

'You saved him from growing into a nasty old man. If you hadn't written how you felt in your note, he wouldn't have learned something new.'

'What was that?'

'To let go.'

'Like me with the kitten?'

I nodded. *And something else you did too*, I thought, as I held her against me. Asking for stories all the time had helped me through that shadowy land to see Liana as she was, to remember the love, and the stuff we'd shared, without that aching pain of loss.

'I'm me now.' It took me a moment to register what Kerra had said.

'What do you mean?'

'I don't want to be Princess Noori or Mariama anymore.' I kissed the top of her head as I thought about her simple, 'I'm me.' She was right. It reminded me of what Zack's grandmother had said. *When you get rid of the illusions hiding what's true, and start believing who you are, the real you comes into focus at last.*

'You have your own special story,' I said.

20

I was packing my bag. It was the story of my life; even as a kid I was always packing, either for boarding school in Pakistan or for holidays at home in the village where Mum and Dad worked. Kerra was out with her dad and Matt had already been in to wish me well with his casual outback charm, so it startled me when I heard the quiet knock on the door.

'How about a ride?' I saw the appeal mixed with excitement in Blake's eyes and before he even explained I knew where we'd go. Apparently he'd been packing too—sausages, damper dough, the billy—while I'd been closeted in my room all morning. It didn't take long to pull on Mrs Townsend's boots and hat.

We'd just reined in at the gorge and I said without thinking, 'This time we'll get to eat it, hey?' For a second I held my breath, remembering all I'd said when we were there before and I waited for his retort as he turned in the saddle to look at me. But it didn't come. He appeared beside Rainmaker, lifting me down the way he used to at my riding lessons and I felt the hardness of his buckle brush against me as he lowered me to the ground, heard his sigh before he spoke.

'I'm sorry about the last time we were here.' I looked away. It wasn't only his fault. I burned inside remembering the times I'd baited him, wouldn't let him alone, thinking I was helping. How much of it was caught up in my own feelings about Liana's death, I may never know. There were things I wished I'd never said at all.

'So am I. It wasn't just you.' I was aware of him then, just like always. It wasn't a sensation I could describe. It wasn't a smell or an image or sound, it was just *there,* inside my middle, exciting, yet it hurt because there was too much of it and I was scared he might not feel it too.

'C'mon.' And I was being led to the ruins by the creek and the antique silent windmill that had no water to pump. It didn't take him long to set up our picnic. He even spread his hands, as he did last time, inviting me to eat, except I wasn't about to ruin it.

'Thanks for this. For inviting me.' *Giving me a second chance.* It sounded inadequate; I meant much more.

He smiled. 'It's okay. Your riding's really improved.' That sounded unrelated but I knew what he meant. Without me learning to ride, we couldn't have done any of it. And I tried to do the picnic justice. Guys can provide so much food and expect you to be able to deal with it. Eating was the last thing on my mind.

'Jaime—' I looked up to find him regarding me. 'I'm sorry about not supporting you enough with your friend Liana. It's just that it reminded me of Mum all over again. It was better to keep quiet. I was a wimp.'

I reached over and touched his hand. 'It's okay, I understand now. What do you think will happen?' I was nearly finished my sausage and damper, taking my time so I wouldn't have to have another. He knew what I meant; just finding Kerra and giving her a ring wasn't going to heal all their hurts.

'Matt and Richelle will manage Mulga Spring for a while. Dad'll come to Adelaide with me and bring Kerra.'

'For counselling?'

He nodded. 'For all of us. I guess there's always hope.'

'Sounds like what Mr Kimberley, my music teacher, said to me after Liana died. Hope isn't a way out, it's a way through. Your family will make it, Blake.'

He finished his sausage then, licked the sauce off his fingers and poured tea from the billy into mugs. 'Thanks,' he said as he handed me one.

'What for?'

'Hanging in there. Sticking with me—when I acted like a jerk.' His words conjured up an image of Richelle, saying how I'd stirred everything up, made trouble.

'Richelle did too.'

'Yeah, but she's my mate. She doesn't have to think about whether she can put up with me for the rest of her life. There's no personal stake in it, no skin off her nose, what I do really.'

I sat there, the enamel mug suspended between the ground and my face. What on earth was he trying to say? And I wanted him to explain but he began packing up the frypan, dousing the coals. He couldn't keep still and for one horrible moment it felt like that other picnic. It was all those feelings about Kerra that drove him that time. This time I hadn't done anything to set him off, so what was wrong? Then he turned to me, his hands full of plates and uneaten damper.

'But with you, Jaime, it's different.'

I swallowed the mouthful of tea I took an aeon ago. 'It is?'

'Yeah.' Suddenly he was in front of me, the plates gone, putting my mug on the ground and drawing me up to face him.

I searched his eyes. It was as though there was so much more he wanted to say, that maybe a guy like him would never say, yet I knew it was there, comforting and warm. Like he was sorry for keeping a distance between us; that now he'd let Kerra in, there was more room for me.

'Jaime?'

'Yes?' Did I say that aloud? I was so intent on not missing his words that I'd held my breath.

'I'm sorry about a lot of things.' And this time when he drew me in against him, I knew what would happen. I could see it in his eyes, in the way he glanced down at my mouth, and this time there was no pain or the salty taste of goodbye. Once I'd asked Dad how I would know when I was in love. He just said I'd know instinctively and I'd said what a cop out. But I understood what he meant now; an unfurling inside told me that this picnic in the gorge with Blake could be a beginning, not an end. Yet I didn't know that when I first met him, not even at the Year 12 dinner the year before. I stood back from him, remembering.

'Do you know, it's over a year since we first met in the library at school and you thought I was…different. Now look at us.' All of a sudden I felt shy.

'They say first impressions stick. You were wrong, you know.'

'About what?'

He bent down to pick up the mugs, the billy, the plates again. It seemed all that 'face to face' stuff was too much for him too, and it wasn't until he put the last things in his saddle bag that he flung the answer back over his shoulder as though it was an after-thought. I knew better.

'About not being a princess from the Himalayas or special.' He remembered saying that? 'And if you come again, I'll take you up over Lake Eyre to see our famous Marree Man. Bet the salt will look just as good as the snow on the Himalayas.'

He led Cador and Rainmaker over. 'You need to see Uluru too. I went with Mum. She called it the heart of Australia, and you know what? When I put my hand on the rock, I could feel it beating.' My eyes widened at his raw honesty inviting me inside.

He smiled uncertainly as he held out Rainmaker's bridle. I'd never thought anything could compare with the Karakorum Mountains or my life in Pakistan. Pakistan would never leave me. There were physical reminders too: kids at school said I had a weird accent and I liked to wear flowing clothes. I'd be embarrassed to be kissed in public, or upset if there was bombing in Afghanistan or Iraq, and I'd sign petitions to free asylum seekers. But I decided Australia was my home, even if I might never fit the mould of what Kate Sample thought was a normal Australian.

As I took the bridle, I felt as if I was accepting more than a strip of leather and a fast ride; that as it warmed in my fingers I was allowing a future within a country that I was learning to love. There was a chance to be myself, wherever I was, even if I'd been raised in two worlds and was living beyond their borders, and possibly always would.

Maybe Blake realised more was going through my head than I could explain as after we'd mounted, he leaned over from his saddle and gently kissed my forehead.

He smiled. 'Kerra'll be waiting. Race you home.'

Acknowledgements

Finding Kerra is a work of fiction and the characters are not based on real people. Thank you to Rochelle Manners who believed Jaime's story was worth reading and for Emily Lighezzolo, my lovely editor, for your helpful suggestions.

Thank you to Gordon, Lyn, Adam, Sarah and Ellen Litchfield of Wilpoorinna Station for your hospitality many years ago. Thanks also to Colin Moulden, Andrea O'Connell, Tim and Sam Prior.

Nazzi's Indigenous proverb 'We are all visitors' can be found at Indigenous Works at www.indigenousworks.ca/en/resources/articles-reports/fire-and-dream.

The original story of 'Nano Begal' (Begal's Mother) that Jaime changes for Kerra can be found in Erik L'Homme (2007). *Tales of a Lost Kingdom: a Journey into NW Pakistan.* NY: Enchanted Lion Books.

The story Jaime tells about Hamid and his sister is based on *Prince Hamid and the Fairy.* (n.d.). Brighton: Litor Publishers.

The full story of 'The Mysterious Traveller' is found in Mal Peet & Elspeth Graham (2011). *Painting out the Stars.* London: Walker Books. The mention of this beautiful story and Jaime's short telling of it to Kerra is used with permission. Thank you, Walker Books Australia.

About the Author

Rosanne Hawke is a South Australian author of 30 books, among them, *Zenna Dare*, *Mustara*, shortlisted in the 2007 NSW Premier's Literary Awards, *The Messenger Bird*, winner of the 2013 Cornish Holyer an Gof Award for YA literature, and *Taj and the Great Camel Trek*, winner of the 2012 Adelaide Festival awards. Rosanne was an aid worker in Pakistan and the United Arab Emirates for ten years and now teaches creative writing at Tabor Adelaide. In 2015 she was the recipient of the Nance Donkin Award for an Australian woman author who writes for children and YA.

More from Rosanne Hawke

Beyond Borders : Dear Pakistan

Jaime Richards has spent most of her life in Pakistan and returning to Australia seems like another planet compared to the country she has left behind. Here in Australia, boys try to kiss her, men wear shorts and everyone says 'cool' all the time. How will she ever know the right things to say or do or wear? After all, this is meant to be her culture.

This is a story of living beyond borders, and discovering the gift of adapting to new cultures, especially one's own.

Beyond Borders : The War Within

Taken at gunpoint into Afghanistan, Jaime and her friends are caught up in a shadowy secret world of intrigue and terrorism. Will they escape the Mujahadeen fighting their holy war?

For Jaime, this trip is to prove painful enough to change her life forever, yet rest the ghosts of her past.

Beyond Borders : Liana's Dance

After her international high school in Northern Pakistan is attacked by terrorists, sixteen-year-old Liana Bedford and the young music and dance teacher, Mikal Kimberley must find a way to rescue student hostages who have been imprisoned in an ancient caravanserai. Liana discovers Mr Kimberley has a secret and to save him and her friends she must overcome her fears and dance for her life.

This is Liana's story as told by her friend Jaime Richards from *Dear Pakistan* and *The War Within.*